The Mysterious Package Company

YOU ARE THE DETECTIVE

POST MORTEM LOS ANGELES
LIGHTS, CAMERA, MURDER!
The Mysterious Package Company

Published by: The Mysterious Package Company

DISCLAIMER:
Post Mortem's story and characters are fictitious. Certain long-standing institutions, agencies, and public offices are mentioned, but the characters involved are wholly imaginary. Any resemblance to actual persons, living or dead, is purely coincidental.

Distributed by:
The Mysterious Package Company
595 Bloorcourt P.O.
Toronto, ON, M6H 1L0

NOTE TO READER:

DO NOT READ
THIS BOOK
FROM BEGINNING
TO END.

AND

READ THE RULES FIRST.

"Hollywood is a place where they'll pay you a thousand dollars for a kiss and fifty cents for your soul."

— Marilyn Monroe

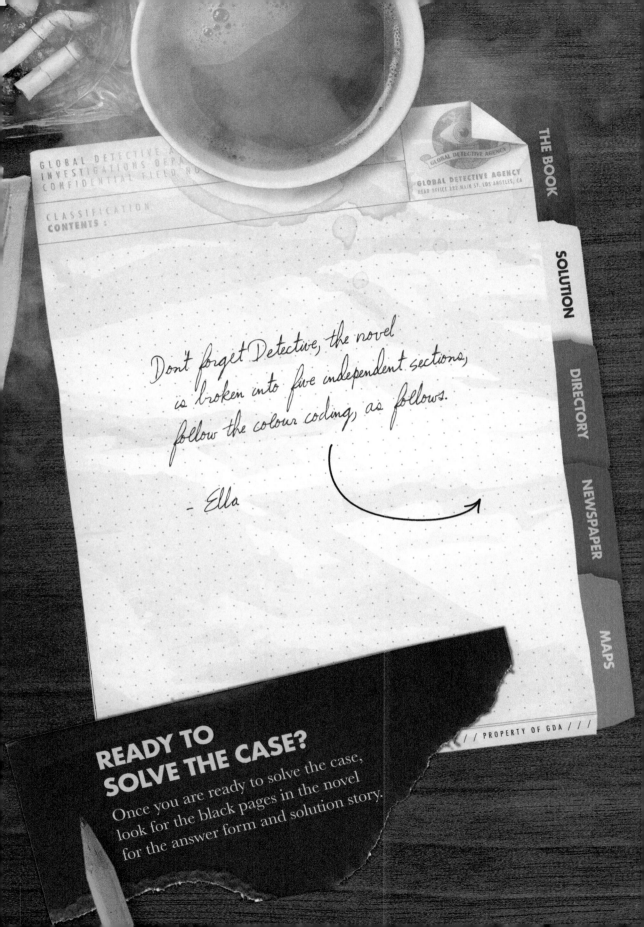

GLOBAL DETECTIVE A
INVESTIGATIONS DEP
CONFIDENTIAL FIELD N

GLOBAL DETECTIVE AGENCY
HEAD OFFICE 222 MAIN ST, LOS ANGELES, CA

CLASSIFICATION.
CONTENTS :

Don't forget Detective, the novel
is broken into five independent sections,
follow the colour coding, as follows.

- Ella

READY TO SOLVE THE CASE?

Once you are ready to solve the case,
look for the black pages in the novel
for the answer form and solution story.

NEW YORK
LOS ANGELES
CHICAGO

LONDON
PARIS
CAIRO

GLOBAL DETECTIVE AGENCY

LOS ANGELES HEAD OFFICE

Dear Agent,

Thank you for your assistance on this case.

During this stage of your employment, YOU are a detective at the Global Detective Agency. As such, you have been granted full security clearance, including access to all crime scenes and witnesses.

You will find the case enclosed. It should be fairly straightforward. You are expected to conduct your own investigation in an independent fashion: Question suspects. Examine evidence. Explore the city. All applicable records and case-files will be made available to you. Upon conclusion, of course, you will be required to fill out a Final Report(Form 15a).

As you surely know, both your letter of recruitment and your GDA badge is required to access our Los Angeles auxiliary offices. Your desk has already been assigned. Coffee remains 2 cents.

Best of luck on your new case. Do whatever you deem necessary, but also keep in mind: *Our eyes never sleep.*

Ella Crane
Ella Crane
Investigations Director

THE RULES

THIS BOOK IS NOT MEANT TO BE READ FRONT TO BACK. ONCE YOU HAVE READ THROUGH THE RULES, PLEASE CONTINUE TO THE INTRODUCTION PAGE TO BEGIN YOUR INVESTIGATION.

INVESTIGATE LEADS

After the Introduction, entries in *The Book* begin with a three-digit Lead at the top of the page. Leads are uncovered as you investigate and can be found on the Map, in the Directory, or at other points during your investigation. If no entry exists when searching out a Lead, you have gone too far off the trail – return to your notes.

Leads for People and Businesses are found in the Directory. There are some Leads that can only be found by questioning suspects, searching your Map, or examining evidence.

Leads can instruct you to take an action:

"Open Evidence A."

Leads can help you decide which lead to pursue next:

"Do you jump from the Roof (123) or dive through the Fire (456)?"

If your investigation has gone dry, your **Informants** might get you back on track. Your list of regular Informants is written inside the cover of the Directory.

Leads always end with the ☛ icon – if you don't see this, there may be more to the Lead on the following page.

EVIDENCE

Discover and unlock evidence throughout the case when prompted, identified by a letter. Once a piece of evidence is revealed, take note and you may access it at any time. Accessing evidence without being prompted to do so is considered cheating! If you investigate a Lead in *The Book* that reveals evidence, you will be instructed ("**Open Evidence A**") which will reveal the evidence on the adjoining page.

DIRECTORY

Right from the beginning of your investigation you will have access to the Directory section of this book by following the **Teal** tabs. People and Businesses in the city are listed here. The three-digit number is a Lead that can be found in *The Book*. The alphanumeric characters are coordinates which correspond to the Map.

NEWSPAPER

You will also have immediate access to the Newspaper section of this book by following the **Brown** tabs. As a detective it's your responsibility to stay informed of current events. Everyday news could be pivotal to your investigation.

MAP

Additionally, you will find two Maps of the Los Angeles area located at the back of this book that are available to you from the outset. The maps are found by following the **Red** tabs. Leads are represented on the Map as a point which contains a three-digit number. If the Lead is significant to the case there will be a corresponding entry in *The Book*. Informants are marked on the Map as stars.

READY TO SOLVE?

To close your case, answer the question found in **Final Report Form 15a** located in the **Solution** section of this book. This section of the book is accessible by flipping to the all black pages of the book.

Once you are satisfied with your investigation, flip the book upside down and continue onto the **Solution**.

KEEP NOTES

As a detective it is critical that you make notes throughout your investigation – you never know what information will be important in solving the case. It is also imperative to document and keep track of which evidence you've uncovered in the back most pages of this novel. Cut out the note pages if it helps make the investigation easier.

**Are you ready to start
Lights, Camera, Murder!?**

TURN THE PAGE TO BEGIN

INTRODUCTION

001

Sunlight sparkles in the midday haze as you drive through the City of Angels, then onto the backlot of Orpheum Pictures. It's like entering some childhood fever dream: A wild west town next to a Chinese temple, then army barracks, then an alien planet. You park beside a tinfoil spaceship as a patrolman approaches.

"I'm with the Agency," you say, pulling out your GDA credentials and stepping onto the surface of Mars. "Can you point me to the crime scene?"

He's young, maybe a rookie, but he's already got that LAPD edge — like he doesn't give a damn, about you or your papers. He hands them back with a snort.

Since the corruption scandal broke, things in L.A. have been tense — even more so now with the district attorney having hired the Global Detective Agency to keep an eye on the cops. They have to cooperate, but they don't have to like it.

"The Atlanta set," says the kid, waving his hand dismissively. "Past the Sahara, the Speakeasy and the Boondocks."

You nod, and walk through Tinseltown — trying to control the nerves you've been feeling since the dispatch: *"Gunshots at Orpheum Pictures Studio. Two victims found on set..."*

The first responding officer, Hickman, is an old-school cop

somewhat brusque and surly. "This way," he says, as you push through a gaggle of coppers and medics. There on the ground are the bodies, like grisly punctuation: the man an exclamation point, his hat at your feet; the woman crumpled and curved, her shape a death-sized question mark.

"Clara Rose," says Hickman.

"The movie star?"

"The very same. And that stiff right there is Joe Fletcher. Ex-husband. Ex-big shot. Ex-pretty much everything by the looks of it..."

On the ground between their hats, like a stray comma in the dirt, lies a Smith and Wesson .45 service revolver. Same as you used to carry. Same as every beat cop and hood from here to the Mississippi.

"Murder weapon?" you ask, pointing to the gun.

Hickman gestures at a giant cannon at the edge of the film set: "Well, that sure ain't it."

"What are they shooting here?" The cannon looks real. The tree looks fake. The noose hanging from it looks dangerous.

"They just wrapped some big Civil War flick. Miss Rose, mind you, wasn't in it. She was working on the Jungle set — other side of the lot: *Leopard People* or some such trash. Don't know what she was doing over here... Other than dying that is. The director found 'em." He checks his notes. "Emmanuel Long. It's in my report."

You look around. You'll have to investigate the whole damn film lot, the whole studio, maybe even the surrounding streets. You're thinking about going to grab the maps from your car, but decide to focus on the crime scene first; it makes sense to explore the surrounds after. You walk a circle around the bodies, noting what's here: Signs of a struggle around Clara's body. Footprints on the hard ground. Three sets of them. Two hats. One gun. Really not much else. "They were found like this?"

"That's right," says Hickman. "We took the photos. Did the interviews. Wrote the report. No one saw anything. But they did hear shots. One, then another. Classic murder-suicide. Open and shut, if you ask me."

You pull on some gloves and start to examine the bodies. Fletcher is face down. When you turn him over you gag for a moment, looking at his mouth — or lack-thereof. The bullet has blown his teeth right through his head. It's like looking at a man who tried to bite his own brain.

"What I tell you?" says Hickman. "Classic."

You pat down Fletcher's pockets, and find a set of car-keys. You hold them up for Hickman to see. "Is there an automobile that goes with these..?"

"No idea."

"So Fletcher just walks – or drives an invisible car – onto a closed set with a gun, first thing in the morning, and shoots his movie star wife?"

"Ex-wife."

You stand up and put the keys into your pocket. "Where the heck is security?"

Hickman shrugs. "Orpheum's got only one guard assigned today – a Frank Figone. He's who called the police. Just read the report, will ya?"

You step over to the body of Clara Rose. It looks as if she's been shot in the heart. You notice something clutched in her right fist. Using your pen and two gloved fingers you gently pry open her hand. There is an open locket. On one side there is a picture of Clara Rose herself — a very alive, very beautiful, young woman. On the other side, dug into the tarnished silver, as if by hand long ago, it reads: *The third of April.*

"What… what day is it today?"

"Saturday," says Hickman.

You tuck the locket back into her hand and stand up.

"I mean the date." But you already know. "April third. Isn't it?"

You take off your gloves, staring down: a blood-stained question at your feet.

Open the report documents and Evidence A

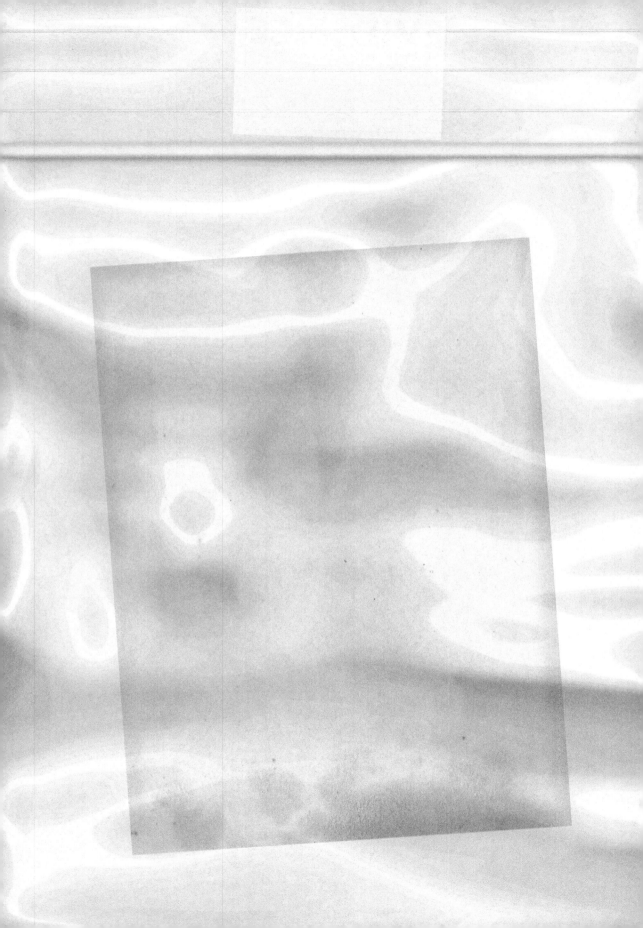

CITY OF LOS ANGELES
CALIFORNIA

OFFICE OF THE
CHIEF OF POLICE

INCIDENT REPORT STATEMENT

DEPARTMENT OF
POLICE
CITY HALL
LOS ANGELES 12
MICHIGAN 5211

IN REPLYING PLEASE GIVE
OUR REFERENCE

049-1948

Hickman, Albert

Saturday April 3 my shift begins at 7:00 am. Call in on a 10-41 -- first
responding officer of a possible "187" at the Orpheum Pictures backlot in
Culver City. Arrive at the lot approximately 10:15 am. Met by private security
guard Frank Figone who had made the call. Large crowd outside movie trailers.
I ascertain that we're still some 300 yards from crime scene and request that
all studio employees and guests remain near trailers. Taken by FF to director
Emmanuel Long, who discovered the crime scene. EL reports hearing two shots. Walk
to vic location, "Civil War Set" guided by EL.

Approaching from the east, two bodies, heads facing west, feet east. possible
murder weapon: Smith and Wesson .45 on ground between vics. Note movie prop tree,
prop antique cannon, pile of lumber, ground combination of grass, gravel and dirt.
Upon close inspection of hard dirt see vague evidence of multiple footprints.

Male vic clearly dead from massive head trauma indicating gunshot. The woman
appears to have died from gunshot to chest. I confirm the witness Emmanuel
Long's actions upon discovering the scene: he says he checked the pulse of the
woman, placed his jacket over her head and returned to administration to call
the police. I remove the jacket but do not otherwise disturb scene. EL identifies
vics as movie star Clara Rose and ex-husband Joe Fletcher. EL reports Alice
Doone as last to have seen Miss Rose alive. EL says AD and others heard shots,
too. I request EL to return to the trailers to manage studio staff. I establish a
perimeter and wait for other units to arrive.

No known witnesses to the crime itself.

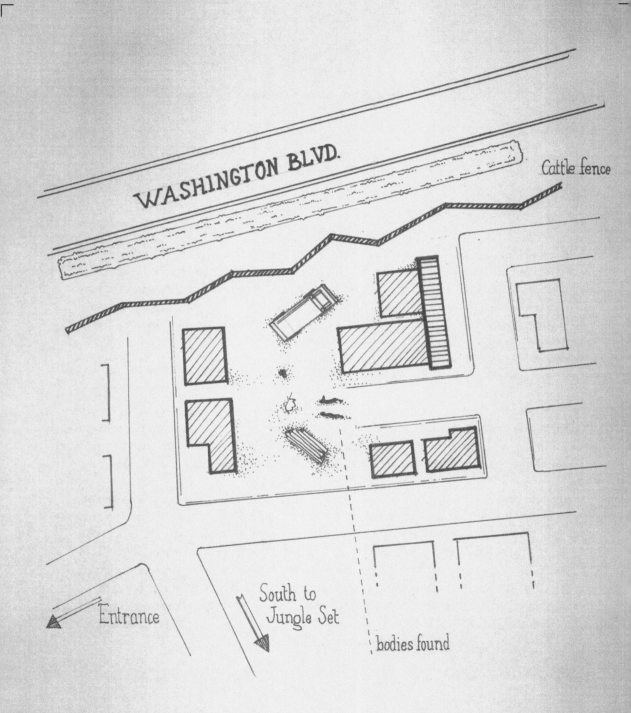

COUNTY OF LOS ANGELES   DEPARTMENT OF CORONER

OFFICE OF THE MEDICAL EXAMINER
AUTOPSY REPORT
CASE REPORT

CASE NO: **049-1948**

APPARENT MODE: Murdered

SPECIAL CIRCUMSTANCES: Celebrity

DECEDENT ROSE, CLARA LEIGH   ROSE, CLARA
LAST, FIRST MIDDLE   AKA

RACE White   SEX F   DOB 3-13-1912   AGE 36   HGT 64 in   WGT 128 lbs.   EYES Brown   HAIR Blonde

INFORMATION ABOUT OCCURRENCE

TYPE OF DEATH Gunshot

PLACE OF DEATH / PLACE FOUND Orpheum Pictures   Culver City
ADDRESS OR LOCATION   CITY

DATE OF DEATH 4-3-1948   TIME 10:25   PRONOUNCED BY Nolan Graves

---

ANATOMICAL SUMMARY:

CLOTHING AND PERSONAL EFFECTS:
Khaki, safari-style pants and white short-sleeved button-down shirt. Beige pith
helmet. Blood on pants and shirt. Scuffed, brown knee-high boots. Leopard-print
scarf around neck. Small purse was found in pants pocket, containing billfold,
lipstick, small change, a small pencil, and house keys. Silver locket and chain
found in right hand.

AUTOPSY:
The body is a 36-year-old white female. Height is 5' 4", weighing 128 lbs. Lividity
is towards the victim's left side and fixed.

Circular perforating entry wound 2" left of center, 4" below clavicle. Abrasion
collar present and uniform, absent of soot deposition or powder stippling.

Autopsy reveals penetrating wound through the left breast, between second and third
rib, through the lung, heart, and carotid artery. Single bullet was recovered at
vertebrae T5.

Bullet is .44 or .45 caliber, badly deformed copper jacket hollow point. Weight
13.8g.

CAUSE OF DEATH:
Gun shot causing arterial hemorrhage.

MANNER:
Trajectory is typical of homicide.

DEC. ROSE, CLARA LEIGH

CASE NO: **049-1948**

DOD 4-3-1948

BODY DIAGRAM
Adult

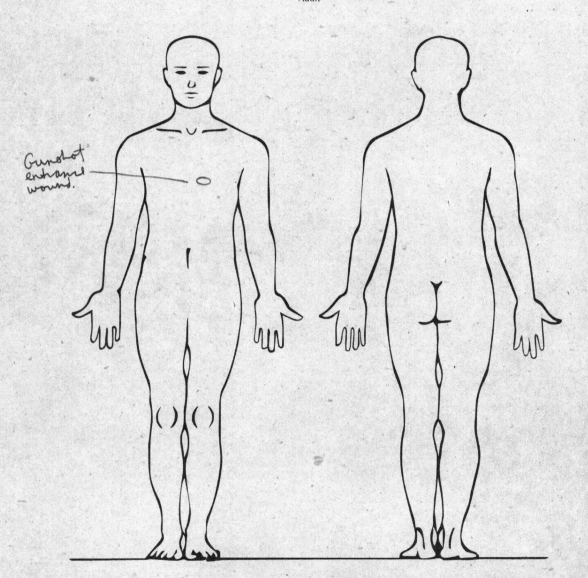

Gunshot entrance wound.

CONCLUSION OR RECOMMENDATION:

I hereby certify that on the 3 day of April 19 48
I made an autopsy on the body of Rose, Clara L.
and upon investigation of the essential facts concerning the circumstances of the
death and history of the case, I am of the opinion that the cause of death was
gunshot to the chest

Date 3 april 1948

Nolan Graves

Deputy Medical Examiner

OFFICE OF THE MEDICAL EXAMINER

AUTOPSY REPORT
CASE REPORT

CASE NO: **049-1948**

| APPARENT MODE: Murdered

| SPECIAL CIRCUMSTANCES: None

ECEDENT FLETCHER, JOSEPH JAMES
      LAST, FIRST MIDDLE   AKA

ACE White   SEX M   DOB 4-9-1901   AGE 47   HGT 71 in   WGT 230 lbs.   EYES Blue   HAIR Brown

INFORMATION ABOUT OCCURRENCE

YPE OF DEATH Gunshot

ACE OF DEATH / PLACE FOUND Orpheum Pictures   Culver City
              ADDRESS OR LOCATION   CITY

ATE OF DEATH 4-3-1948   TIME 10:25   PRONOUNCED BY NOLAN GRAVES

ANATOMICAL SUMMARY:

CLOTHING AND PERSONAL EFFECTS:
Grey tweed coat. Brown straw fedora with striped band. Black dress pants. Blue
dress shirt. Black wing-tipped brogue dress shoes. Wallet found in pocket
contained driving license and empty billfold. Small change found in separate
pocket.

AUTOPSY:
The body is a 47-year-old hispanic male. Height is 5' 11', weighing 230 lbs.
Lividity is anterior and fixed.

The subject presents with an asymmetrical upper lip and shattered maxilla
displacing multiple teeth. Soot deposition is present on the nose, nostrils,
cheeks, lips, tongue and hard palate. Perforating entry wound with long abrasion
collar present on hard palate. Two teeth embedded in hard palate match heavy
staining of the deceased.

Shallow bruising on right hand knuckles, three to five.

Autopsy confirmed perforating entry wound into the skull. Soot and powder
deposition are present in brain tissue. Recovered multiple tooth fragments. Bullet
exited rear of skull from right occipital.

No bullet recovered from crime scene.

CAUSE OF DEATH:
Gunshot to the mouth.

MANNER:
Trajectory is typical for suicide, at the very least close contact with the face.
But noted some powder residue on hands. And incongruous burn marks on face.

DEC. FLETCHER, JOSEPH JAMES

CASE NO: **049-1948**

DOD 4-3-1948

BODY DIAGRAM
Adult

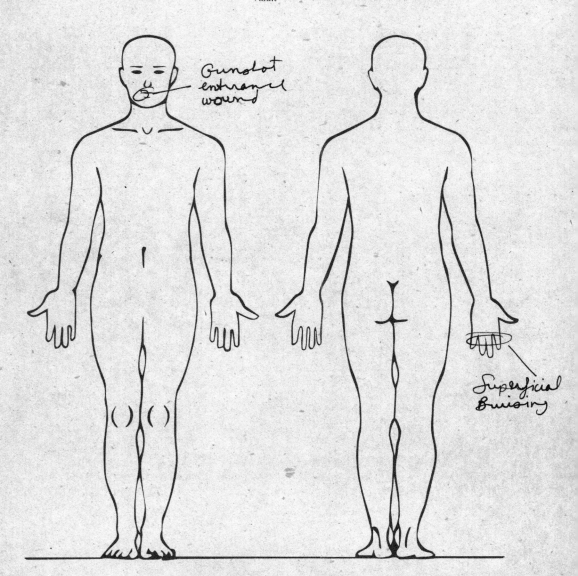

Gunshot entrance wound

Superficial Bruising

CONCLUSION OR RECOMMENDATION:

I hereby certify that on the 3 day of April 19 48
I made an autopsy on the body of Fletcher, Joseph J
and upon investigation of the essential facts concerning the circumstances of the
death and history of the case, I am of the opinion that the cause of death was
gunshot to the mouth

Date 3-April-1948

Nolan Graves

Deputy Medical Examiner

REMINDER TO
INVESTIGATOR:

_____

*DO NOT READ
THIS BOOK
FROM BEGINNING
TO END.*

**GOOD LUCK,
DETECTIVE.**

**IT IS TIME TO
BEGIN YOUR
INVESTIGATION.**

010

The famous Ella Crane sits like a poised viper in the inner-sanctum of her GDA headquarters. The shocked faces of long-dead, possibly tortured, animals stare down at you like ghosts. You assume she beheaded them herself.

"How is your progress?" she asks, her unblinking eyes magnified through horn-rimmed glasses.

"Um..." you say, searching for a feasible answer. The grandfather clock ticks from the corner, as she stares into your soul. You were planning on asking for leads, but that seems foolish now... There are stories about Ella Crane, going back nearly a century: how she was a sniper in the Union Army, tracked down John Wilkes Booth, buried Custer with her bare hands...

Suddenly she is up, facing a painting on the wall to your left. "Who, pray tell, is this?" she asks.

"Uh," you say, and take a breath. "That's Dugald T. Geddes, the founder of the Agency."

"And what, pray tell, is our credo?"

"Our eyes never sleep." You say it quick and automatic, like she's holding a pistol to your head.

"And what, pray tell, does that mean?"

"It means... um, they're always open... our eyes... never close...?"

She is back in her chair.. The unblinking is unnerving. You're in the trance of her pupils now... *never close, never close...*

"You!" she says, snapping your attention. "Are making an inauspicious start. You are making an inauspicious start to your probationary period. You. Are making. An inauspicious start. To your probationary. Period. On a potentially sensitive matter. Need I continue?"

"No. No," you say. It feels like you're being bludgeoned by

her clauses.

"Now, from the outset this looks like a murder-suicide, no?"

"No. I mean yes. I mean, it might be."

"Well, why don't you start there?"

"Um… where?"

"Anywhere. But. Here."

You nod, stand, bow, tip your hat, nod again, then weave out of the office like a punch-drunk lightweight. ◢

011

There is a loading dock at the rear of the Hall of Justice. It is through here that the daily dozen-or-so — be they rich or poor, loved or loathed, famous or nameless — arrive for one last taste of L.A. hospitality.

Among the sorry stiffs, deputy coroner Nolan Graves is munching an egg-salad sandwich, scrutinizing a textbook. He looks up as you approach.

"Here for the Orpheum case?"

"Sure."

"You can have the news before the cops do. Dame was killed; one shot, right here." He taps his chest, "but the gent..." He slides off his stool, taking another bite of the sandwich, and draws your attention toward two shrouded slabs. Without warning, he lifts a sheet covering the remains of Joe Fletcher's face, speaking around a knot of food in his cheek, "Everything matches the .45 you found."

"Suicide?" you say, trying to avoid the sight of either man's mouth.

"Well that's the funny part..." says Graves.

You're well aware that coroners have a unique concept of "funny," and so you wait while he finishes chewing.

"... The angle fits. But see this?" He traces a circle with the pinky of his sandwich hand, hovering over the crater of flesh and teeth. "If you're going to shoot yourself in the face, you stick the barrel in your mouth. This guy's got burns all over his face."

You let out a low whistle.

"Didn't spot it at the scene, huh?" He lets the sheet drop.

"Well, you *are* pretty green." His brow knits. "Hickman, on the other hand — he's ripe as they come... Maybe he got distracted."

"Or maybe," you say. "He wanted this to be easy."

"They all want that. Every time." Graves returns to his desk, and the other half of his sandwich. "It warms my heart, to complicate their lives..."

Between the bodies and his desk is a large tray containing the victim's personal effects. You glance them over, and pick up the locket that was clenched in Clara's fist. *Why not around her neck?* you wonder.

She looks so young in your hands, so lovely. But already, somehow torn. And the etching, with today's date, causes you to shiver.

"What do you make of this?"

"Another complication," smiles Nolan, and takes a bite of his sandwich. ◢

012

As Trudy walks you through the concrete labyrinth, beneath the Agency headquarters, you keep your focus on her. It would be difficult, complicated, and probably disastrous to separate Trudy from the Repository. They are both the blood-lines of the Agency's knowledge: serpentine, vital, and musty.

When she gets to her desk, in the center of the catacombs, Trudy turns to face you. "Clara Rose and Joe Fletcher," she says. "Correct?"

You hazard a nod.

She slips in behind her desk, pulls a pencil from the silver bun of her hair, writes Clara's name, one block letter at a time, onto a yellow form, followed by a flurry of swirls. She rolls the paper, sticks the paper in a capsule, the capsule up into a pneumatic tube. You watch as it flies like a rocket. And by the time you look back at Trudy, she's turned to this morning's crossword.

"Nimbus," you say.

"I'm sorry?"

"41 down." You point at the puzzle, "Six-letter word for a stormy cloud."

Thunk. A tube lands behind her, and Trudy pulls it out. She removes the paper, unfurls it and reads: "I'm sorry it looks like both parties were born out of state, we won't have any early records for either. We have a record of ongoing separation proceedings though. Clara Rose's lawyer is one Stephen Costa. Fletcher appears to be without council." She glances up. "Might that help?"

"It might," you say. "Thank you." ◢

013

Auxiliary agents are stationed in the Bradbury building, three blocks from GDA headquarters — just far enough that it's a bit of a walk, and close enough that you'll be reprimanded for taking a cab. You could take your own car, though parking will flip your lid.

The Bradbury has many layers, all of them inscrutable — brown brick façade, five-story glass atrium, maze of wood-paneled walkways and iron railings hazily lit, then a birdcage elevator. After that, the layers become levels. And you get off on the fifth.

It is a square, open space, with row upon row of grey tanker desks, punctuated by the occasional water cooler. Banker boxes labeled either "DA" or "GDA" are stacked pretty much everywhere. Affixed to each desk is a brass plate engraved with either a name or number. As a probationary cautionary auxiliary investigator, yours is a number: 23.

There is a file on the desk. The front reads, "Agent 24."

A foot or so to your right, a bald man at another desk is typing. You say hello.

"What do you want?" he says, still typing.

"Nothing, just hello."

"That's all?"

"Well, my desk says 23, and my agent number is 24."

"So?" He continues to type.

"Is that a mistake?"

"The Agency doesn't make mistakes. Are you your desk?"

"Um. I'm not sure."

"You are not sure if you are a desk?"

"No. I'm not."

"You're not sure?"

"I'm not a desk."

"Ok. There you go."

You look at his nameplate.

"But your desk says Feswick. Is that who you are?"

He stops typing. And looks at you. "Are we going to have a problem?"

You look for somewhere to hang your coat. ◢

014

You tap the glass of a first-floor window at the Los Angeles Examiner. Agnes Ross is in the midst of talking, always talking, but she acknowledges you with the jerk of her thumb towards the front door.

Linotypes clatter as you squeeze past the ink-fingered copy-boys, into the sprawl of her office, where some poor syndication stiff is making his final pitch:

"How about the anagrams? Dear Delilah?"

"Twice is my limit, Teddy; don't make me say no again."

"Alright, alright, but at least think about the horoscope..." He slinks past you out the door, utterly defeated.

"Still breaking hearts, I see."

"And yet they keep on coming back. Speaking of which, been a while since you darkened my door." Agnes is short and stocky, but the fastest gal you know.

"Got a new gig," you say.

"Don't I know it. The GDA's new wunderkind."

"Hardly."

"Is there some kind of oath you guys have to take?"

"That's confidential." You flash her a smile.

"Of course it is. Secret handshake?"

You nod. "I'll show it to you someday. In the meantime…"

"Oh, the meantime! Let me guess... Clara Rose."

"You're a crackerjack," you say.

"Sure. And you're a prize. What do you got so far?"

"Honestly?" You take a seat. "Not much I haven't read in the papers."

"And we thank you for your business. But really..." Agnes pulls out a pencil and taps it on her notepad. "Our reporters are going with a murder-suicide. Is there another angle? Did Joe Fletcher not kill Clara Rose?"

Your head begins to ache. "I didn't say that. Look, I'm happy to tell you something when I know it, but I'm still just fact-finding."

"Ah. So you're hoping I have facts?"

"That, or… I don't know. I'm just sort of stuck."

"So," she says, dropping her pencil, "You and your ultra-mysterious Agency want some *advice?* You should try Dear Delilah."

"Thanks for nothing…" You start to stand.

"Oh, don't be such a grouch. What I would do — if I were a young detective — is go back to the crime scene and take a look around, then move farther and farther out. I mean, you have a map, don't you? And you could try concentric circles. Concentric circles, I often find, are really quite calming, sometimes even helpful. You might discover something you weren't even looking for… There. How was that?"

"Always worth the visit," you say, standing up and tipping your hat.

Agnes Ross leans back in her chair. "Now, how about that handshake?" ◣

015

Joe Muzzie's red and yellow DeSoto Taxi weaves through the afternoon traffic as he continues his dissertation on snake-oil-salesmen. His five-day air-freshener is on its 20th month, but sometimes he's got a fresh nugget or two. It's hard to tell if this is going to be one of those times.

"So we use it synonymous with 'grifter,' right? Or 'flim-flam man'. But what if snake oil works? Which it most definitely does… The Chinese folks who built the train-tracks, they're the ones who brought it here — the oil of Chinese water snakes. It killed the pain and swelling, so you can keep on trussing down that line. Yankees got a hold of it, put it in patent medicines, made you feel just fine. Weren't till a huckster named Clark Stanley, the Rattlesnake King — self-styled cowboy, spun snakes in the air like lassos, and sold Stanley's Snake Oil from town to town. FDA seized his wares, put it under their microscopes, and know what they found? They found mineral oil, beef fat, red pepper juice, turpentine — all sorts of sticky stuff — but not one lick of good ol' snake oil. And so 'snake oil salesman' becomes shorthand for goddamn unscrupulous shifty bullcrap — not because the man sold snake oil, but because the man did *not*."

"And what does this have to do with Clara Rose?" you ask, holding your nose against the interior scent.

"Now *that*," says Muzzie, "is a very good question. Did you know they used rats as currency on Easter Island?"

You ask him to pull to the curb. "I think I'll walk from here," you say, forking over a dollar. ◢

016

Edie Elam, among the dozen Hollywood souls who could make or break one's career, is perhaps the only one beholden to no one — neither the studios nor the mob. Even the papers give her free reign. And she takes her power seriously, though you might not know it from the gossip columns. Her legions of readers think she's dishing and dishing, shooting from the hip, then dishing some more. And they just can't get enough.

"Sit down," she says, as you approach the booth at the Russo Supper Club. It's obvious she has no time for niceties, let alone appetizers.

"Clara was one of the good ones," she says, as you slide across the bench. "She was a good person, and a good actress. And if you're here for the right reasons, I want to help you out."

"I appreciate that. Can you tell me…"

"Listen," says Edie, looking you in the eye. "I want to make sure I've got your attention."

You nod.

"Instead of all the rigamarole about whatever questions you might have prepared — in the handful of hours since you showed up at Orpheum — can we just take for granted that I'm pretty sure what they'd be, and skip to the part where I'm genuinely trying to help you…?"

You nod once more.

"Okay. All of this is for you, and no one else. Take very good notes. And then make sure to lose them. You understand?"

Yet another nod.

"Okay. Here we go. Clara was a good person with a broken heart." She stares at you expectantly. "Why aren't you writing that down? I know the difference between gossip and facts. It's what I deal in. I give away the gossip for cheap. What I'm giving you is invaluable. If you know how to use it right. Now are you ready this time?"

You assure her you are.

"The people who made Clara a star are the people who destroyed her. I'm not talking about her fans. People think fans choose their stars. It's not even close to that. But I am talking about Clara, too. She's to blame, in part, as well. You should go look for the other parts. But also, know this: There's a big difference between destroying a person and killing them. You've got to keep that in mind."

You look up from your notepad, having a hard time keeping up, but hoping for more.

"You know," says Edie Elam, "What you and I do is pretty much the same. We both gather information, learn things, collect stories. I sell the supposedly valuable stuff that everyone thinks they want — and is, of course, utterly useless. Then I keep what they don't even know about. That way I've got every key. Here's my advice to you, agent-who-still-has-a-soul: If you can learn the true worth of information, and how and where to find it, the only thing left is to keep it under your hat. And then one day, it becomes your dragon."

Your notes have turned into scribbles. You have no idea if this has been helpful, but feel oddly thankful nonetheless. ◢

017

From where you're sitting — at the very back of an otherwise empty theatre — it's hard to tell if *Red-headed Step-child* is supposed to be a comedy, tragedy, horror-flick or snuff film. There's a lot of high-pitched wailing.

Between that and the whirr of the projector it's a challenge to hear what Detective Burlage is saying, which of course is by design. Your inside source on the LAPD is paranoid about being seen with you, let alone heard. And so you end up watching a lot of mediocre matinees together.

"Clara Rose," he whistles. "High profile case. Sounds like they're grooming you."

"I'm sure the precinct is hoping I make a mess of it."

"I'm sure we are."

"What can you tell me?"

He glances at the exits. "I know she's had some troubles. House was robbed, threatening letters..."

"You think those things are connected?"

"Well I'll tell you who is: Clara Rose's business partners. Connected all the way to Cosa Nostra."

A woman on the screen is shrieking. She's wrestling with a mannequin.

"You mean her friends at Orpheum Studios?"

"Maybe them, too. But no." Burlage scans the theatre for the 15th time; you're still the only ones here. "I'm talking about her restaurant: The Sidewalk Café. Gangsters are good for a laugh, sure, until their greasy fingers are sticking in your pie."

A whole chorus-line is screaming now, as the song they were dancing to is drowned out by children in animal masks shooting tommy guns into the sun.

"This really is a terrible movie," you say. "Even more-so than usual." ◢

018

Out of all your informants — even Muzzie — Cecil Neddie makes you the loopiest. But of course beggars who choose are called burglars — which is what Neddie used to be — and you've only got so many snitches to pick from.

"I ain't a snitch," says Neddie. At least you think that's what he's said. It's hard to hear from this phone booth, while he's standing in the one next to you, and neither of the phones are dialed in.

"What?" you say.

"Hold it to your ear!" says, Neddie, gesturing with his own, lifeless telephone receiver. "So people think we're talking."

"We *are* talking!" you say. "We're just not *hearing*, Neddie! Can we get out of the booths and talk?"

"Are you kidding!?" Neddie is hissing a whisper, like he's got laryngitis. "Then our cover's blown.

You take a breath. It's always like this with Neddie. So much work to get hold of so little, usually nothing at all.

"So put in a dime!" you call through the glass. "I'll read you out the number!"

"Why don't *you!*" shouts Neddie. "I don't have a dime!"

You fish through your pockets: Your GDA badge, more like an I.D. card; a half pack of chewing gum, ticket-stubs from last week's late-night wrestling, three paper clips, and your wallet. Your wallet contains a five-dollar bill, a number of business cards, and two photos: one of your loving family, and one of someone you want to forget. You have no dime.

"Good talk," you say, before hanging up. Then you step out of the booth, wave to Neddie, and head towards your car. ◗

019

Emmanuel Long settles into the nook of a cramped Hayes trailer. His hands shake as he lights a smoke: "Jesus H. Christ! I've filmed plenty of death scenes before — even one with Clara Rose. But I was not ready for this. Not one goddamn bit."

"Nonetheless, can you take me through it?"

"Sure I can." You wait as he takes another drag, a long exhale… "She was always wandering off, our Clara. I went to her trailer, she wasn't there. Alice Doone's trailer is next door."

"That's another actress?

"Yeah. Don't you watch the pictures?" Another long drag. "Alice said she'd seen Clara, walking towards the Civil War set. So that's the way I headed. And then I heard the shots."

"Can you describe them?"

"Well, they're always shooting blanks on one set or another. But this sounded different. Or maybe I'm just thinking that now. I dunno. But I swear it felt different, you know: *Boom.* Then *Boom.* One, then another. Then I got there, and saw them on the ground."

"How long after the shots did you get there?"

"I dunno. A minute? Maybe two? I saw it was Clara. And I knew that she was dead. Then I heard Alice Doone screaming behind me: 'She's dead! Oh, my god she's dead!' And that was no acting, I tell you. Alice Doone was panicking. Maybe even in shock. I tried to calm her down, held her. Then I walked her back, quick as we could, to call the cops."

"And what about Fletcher?"

"Didn't even realize it was him till after. That lousy sonafabitch. She should have left him years ago."

"Weren't they divorced?"

"Not that I know. I mean, she called him her Ex. But far as I know, it wasn't official. Guess it's official now…" The director spits out a laugh, and stubs out his smoke. "I should have known something was wrong."`

You ask what he means.

"Clara. She just wasn't herself lately — little squabbles with the cast, the crew, everyone. It wasn't like her. And last night at the club she pretty much picked a fight…"

"You saw this?"

"No. But everyone else in Hollywood did. At least that's how they're talking about it."

You ask what the fight was about.

"No idea. I just hoped she was okay. That's why I wanted to check in before shooting. But of course I couldn't find her — until I did. And she was *not* okay."

"I am sorry. What's going to happen with your movie?"

"*My* movie? I'm just the poor director. You gotta ask the producer about that. You should talk to Overfield anyway. He was on set then, too."

He lights another cigarette, watching the match burn down, wincing as it licks his thumb. "She did not deserve this, our Clara. Not one bit." ▰

029

Walking alongside the gurgling pool, you cross the Sandman parking lot one more time, locate the right number and knock on the door.

When finally he opens, Thomas Deasy is even less impressive than you've come to imagine: average height, average looks, not groomed enough to suggest any style, not rough enough to seem intriguing. The only point of note at all — apart from the dame hiding behind him — is the brand-new, ill-fitting trilby hat sitting atop his head. You take yours off as you step inside.

"Hey!" says the gal. "You can't just come in!"

You look at her — skinny, disheveled, and nervous — and offer up a nod. "Mr. Deasy asked me in. Didn't you, Tom?"

Deasy, still standing where he answered the door, says nothing. The gal says, "Who are you?"

"I am a weary soul," you admit. "Who has had a long day. And could probably do with a drink." You sit down on one of the beds. The gal looks at Deasy, who motions for her to do something. You place your hat next to you.

"Bad luck," says the gal, crossing to the ice-box.

"How's that?"

"A hat on a bed. That's mighty bad juju."

"Oh," you say. "Just for me, or for all of us?"

She shrugs. You do, too, and leave the hat where it is. Tom Deasy stares at it.

When the woman hands you a bourbon and soda, she also reaches out and touches the turkey-egg lump behind your hairline. "Ouch," she says.

You should have been off duty hours ago. And it's really been a helluva day. So you take a sip, put the glass on the windowsill, and prepare to take some notes..

"Now Mr. Deasy — How about Tom instead?" Deasy nods. "Now Mr. Tom." Deasy winces. "You are aware that Clara Rose — your once star client, friend of more than twenty years, and generous employer — was found dead extremely recently, and under curious circumstances."

Deasy nods.

"And you are also aware that your studio-wingman, your brother-in-arms, your fleabag-motel-buddy, and husband of Clara — Mr. Joe Fletcher — was also found dead at the scene?"

You sip your drink. Deasy persists with the nodding.

"And you can probably surmise, that various people connected with law-enforcement, including myself, have been actively concerned with your whereabouts?"

To his nodding he adds a shrug. You notice a colony of small sweat-beads gathering beneath his ill-fitting hatband. You gesture for him to sit down, on the other bed.

"So here's the thing," you say. "I've had all this time now, wondering where you've been, to really think about things. And do you know what I think?"

He opens his mouth, but doesn't come up with words.

"I think I could just go ahead and arrest you now."

The skinny girl with gentle hands lets out a little yelp.

"At least for embezzlement, theft, and fraud. And I doubt your victim being a well-loved, tragically-deceased, sadly-missed, all-American-starlet will help your case very much."

Deasy gets up and pours himself a glass of Scotch, neat.

"And I'm also thinking," you say, "that I could add some more. Extortion, for example. Or what about Blackmail? Really, is there any crime you didn't perpetrate against your dear friend? Oh, and then there's murder, of course. I'd hate to see what you do to your enemies…"

"That's enough!" says Deasy, finally finding his voice. "You've got it all wrong." He slugs down the Scotch, and sits on the bed, staring into his empty glass.

"I had people watching out for her to make sure she was safe."

You let him continue.

"I have a friend at the lot. Well, yeah... She has been reporting back to me."

"Why were you keeping tabs on her Deasy?"

"Because of the threats, she never wanted to talk about them, but I've seen them. These threats were different from the others."

"Who is the informant on the lot?" You ask.

He looks at the gal sheepishly, shakes his head, and takes a long breath. "Penny Andrews. I see her in the evenings and she gives me the updat-"

The gal immediately pounces off the bed and begins shouting, "You said you were done with her, you Pig! You sai-"

You stick out your hand in the general direction of the gal. Your rudeness clearly catches her off guard and she falls silent. "Who were the threats coming from, Deasy?"

"Probably Fletch. He was always extorting her, blackmailing her." He says, now staring down at his socks. "That's what their whole sham marriage was. All those years: one long extortion-blackmail-honeymoon. But she'd finally had enough of it — and he was losing control, and getting desperate. The funny thing: no matter how wrong he might have been, he was still so in love with her. Even more-so after the war. But he was pretty mixed up. We both were, I guess." He turns the glass over and stares at its bottom. "But there was something about Clara — it's hard to explain. It's like she wanted to be used — loved and stepped-on at the same time. I know how that sounds — but it's not an excuse; it's true." He lifts his head, and looks at you. "Sure I took advantage. Everyone did. The café books — you've probably been talking to that weasel, Hall? It wasn't just my doing. It was everyone's doing. And Clara knew about it, at least on some level. She'd go to the wall for just about anyone, except herself. It's like she wanted the punishment. And this whole town can dish out that."

He breathes. Opens his mouth again, then stops.

You ask if Clara was always that way.

"Nope," says Deasy, firmly.

You look at him straight. "Do you know when it changed?"

"Sure do," he says, returning the look. "Down to the day. Even right down to the hour. But that's something I'll never tell. I know you think I did her wrong, and I'm sure I did. But I never broke that promise. And I never used her secrets as threats. Other people did. But that's where I draw the line.... Oh and you should also know: I didn't kill her."

You stand up. "Of course you didn't."

They can't quite tell if you're being sarcastic. You finish your drink, and walk to the door.

"One last question: Do you happen to know a two-headed, red-headed monster?"

"What do you mean?"

"Not entirely sure. Maybe some ginger twins with a habit of hurting people?"

"The Webb Brothers? You must be talking about the Webb Brothers?"

"I guess I must." You open the door. "By the way, the cops will probably be here soon. And also you should call your wife. She misses you." You tip your hat to the skinny girl, and exit into the parking lot.

The swimming pool is bubbling. You step into your car, pop an Aspirin, and merge into the traffic. ◢

035

Through the front-porch screen you see Hickman in his undershirt, striding towards you, already fuming as he reaches the door.

"What the hell are you doing at my house?"

You have no answer for him.

"Is there an issue with the report?"

"Not so much…"

"Then what in God's name do you want?"

"Uh…"

"Uh!? Why don't you go bother McTeague instead."

"McTeague?"

"Yeah. See what happens if you tramp all over *his* lawn. That Mic ain't friendly like me."

"McTeague...?"

"Oh, for Christ's sake!" Hickman slams the door. ◢

037

An elegant iron gate blocks the driveway entrance to Clark Gable's mansion. You try the intercom but get no answer. You press the button a dozen more times before deciding maybe, just maybe, the name in the motel registry was a fake. ◢

045

"She was certainly with us last night," says Farhad, a somewhat fussy, overly polished bar manager at the Trocadero Nightclub. "But anyone could tell you that. Even on her best days, Clara Rose never went unnoticed. And yesterday was *not* her best day."

"Neither was today."

Farhad grimaces. "Ghastly business. Absolutely ghastly. Shot through the heart, they say!"

You take out your notebook. "And what do you say about last night?"

"Well. I'd never want to speak ill of Miss Rose, you understand..."

"Of course not. But if pressed?"

"Hmm… If pressed, I'd say she was in a proper fighting mood last night. And that this mood of hers led to two separate episodes — incidents, really. Incident the first with a woman in a gorgeous dress. Words were shared, tempers flared…"

"This woman in the dress…"

"Emerald green, fabulous gloves - unmistably Rathbuns."

"Ok. Do you happen to know who she was?"

"Indeed I do. If pressed, I'd say she was the wife of William Hale. Mrs. Hale. First name unknown to me."

"And incident the second?"

Farhad whistles, as if calling for curtains to open. "This was a proper scene. Imagine, if you will, sitting at our finest table, the one-and-only Mr. Howard Hughes, and the great — or at least stupendously round — Mr. Otto Friedrich. Then enter Miss Rose, an extra drink on her breath, cheeks as red as her name. She accosts the men — *accost* is the word. And things get out of hand. Not fisticuffs exactly — but mighty close. Spilled champagne and broken glass. Shattered peace and besmirched tranquility. That's what I'd say, if pressed."

"Why those two? Howard Hughes and Otto Friedrich?"

"This whole town revolves around them!" Farhad waves his hand in the air, as if describing the solar system? "In fact, doesn't everything?"

"Well, what was the fight about?"

"That," sighs Farhad. "I could not tell. I try to mind my own business of course."

You nod understandingly. "Then how to did it resolve?"

"It was Ida Lupino who broke them up – sent Clara home with our chauffeur; that's something we do for our special guests. And of course we provided the gentlemen with drinks on the house."

"Very thoughtful. And Ida Lupino!" You make a note. "You do get the stars in here don't you?"

Farhad grins.

"Did you notice anything else? Anything out of the ordinary?"

"Well, no. Except Miss Rose did use the phone at the bar. I do remember that."

You ask when the call took place.

"Between the two incidents – I'm sure of that. 10pm perhaps? It seemed like a tense call. But I'd never listen in, of course."

"Of course, of course. But you might have heard something by accident."

"That I might have," says Farhad, nodding at the distant possibility. "Something perhaps about plans to meet, to meet alone — though not wanting to do it. And needing to keep it on the down-low sly, the QT, the hush-hush – something like that I might have heard. Also heard something about a boardwalk, and rental units, and traveling abroad… maybe even a mention of a door-prize, a racehorse, a baby, a leopard, and someone, oh no, definitely someone named Chuck, or Chet… really I wasn't listening."

"Of course not," you say. "But thank you all the same."

Farhad gives a bow. ◢

088

The Needham Family home is a little bungalow on a pleasant-seeming cul-de-sac. Mr. Needham answers the door. He's also pleasant, but not so little, with a square jaw and hands that look ready for action.

"Hello, Detective," he says. "I know you have a job to do. But Andy has spoken with the police already. He was a minor when the burglaries took place. The victim filed no charges. I am his father, and I'd like him to be left alone."

There's something in his demeanor that reminds you of police-tape and briefings, and your time at the academy…"Reggie Needham? *Detective* Reggie Needham?"

"Nope, Kid," he says, half-smiling. "Not 'Detective' anymore."

Nope is right. The D.A. saw to that. Some of L.A.'s finest had to take the fall: What it meant for Needham was early retirement; not the humiliation others had faced — but not exactly a decorated end to his career either.

"Andy's your boy?" McTeague had left this detail out of the report.

"He's a good kid. Just going through a tough time…" Needham glances down at his feet. "It's ever since his mom died. Cancer. And adolescence." He looks at you and nods. "That's a one-two punch. He won't be breaking in anywhere else. You have my word on it."

Needham has that feel: steely, true and calm — the kind of cop you'd wanted to be.

"I'd still like to talk to him," you say. "It is a murder investigation now. And he might shed some light."

Needham nods, like he knew this would be the case. He leaves you there in the doorway, then reappears with his son.

"Hi," says Andy Needham.

He doesn't look like a criminal, or even a delinquent. Really just a kid. And not a happy one. It seems like he's been crying. His hands shake. You take out the note you got from McTeague. "Can you tell me where you found this, Andy?"

Andy nods, and looks at you. "In Clara Rose's house," he says. You ask him to be more specific. "In her bedroom. In a drawer by her bed."

"Ok," you say, then soften your voice: "Andy, do you know that Clara Rose has died?"

Andy looks stricken, but not in a way that suggests surprise. More like a reminder of grief. His body starts trembling, but it eases when his dad puts a hand on his shoulder.

"You've admitted to burglarizing her residence," you say carefully, in a manner you think Detective Needham would appreciate. "Can you tell me why you did that?"

"I…" You can see he's choking up. "I've seen her movies…" He takes a heavy breath, and looks right through you. "I guess I was just curious."

You lean forward, gaze fixed on Andy. "The number of pieces reported stolen was inconsistent with what was returned. Can you explain what happened to the locket?"

Andy's eyes dart nervously to his father before he answers. "I gave it back to her directly, Detective," his voice shaking slightly.

Detective Needham's expression remains stoic, but you can see the flicker of resentment in his eyes. "I think that's probably enough for now, *Detective*." He says.

You thank them both and leave them there — father and son, looking into the middle distance. ◢

098

Barry Miller, the Sidewalk Café dishwasher, invites you into his small, windowless apartment on Normandie.

"I'll help however I can," he says, shaking your hand with vigor. "I worked for Miss Rose a long time, and always liked that gal, I did — both on and off the screen. Have you seen her motion pictures? They really are a treat."

You ask whether Joe Fletcher had been to the restaurant recently.

"Nah, he doesn't come around. He's still friends with Tom though— he's our bartender. They go back to the good old days — even before the war — when Tom was Clara's agent. That's the thing about this town, you know. Everyone's in the movies."

"So this Deasy fellow," you say. "What's his connection with a Chaz…?"

"Mr. Chaz," says Miller.

"His parents didn't give him a first name?"

"Not so I know. But he's always at the café — walking around like he owns the place. To tell the truth, it's like he's Deasy's real boss, if you know what I mean. Got that Tom under his thumb — Tom Thumb! That's funny, hey? — This one time, I seen Mr. Chaz threaten Deasy just by picking up a kitchen knife real slow like, just turning it over in his hands. Right creepy, if you ask me."

"So he had sway over Deasy, you're saying?"

"Sure. Deasy owes him money, for one thing. That's clear as Doris Day. Though I couldn't tell you what from. Gambling, maybe?"

"Gambling, you say?"

Miller's eyes go wide, like maybe he's said too much.

"It's okay," you tell him. "I know about the tables. You've been a great help, and nothing you say will come back to you."

He breathes a long, audible sigh of relief. ◪

103

Ida Lupino meets you at her favorite café, nodding to the waiter before sliding into the booth. Only then does she take off her dark sunglasses. Her eyes are a startling blue. You can tell she's been crying.

"Is it really true?" she says. "Clara's gone?"

You offer your condolences, and ask how they met.

"I think it was an exec party. Maybe even Friedrich's. A long, long time ago. I was just a kid when we met, and Clara became like an older sister — always trying to protect me. Now look at me. I'm practically over the hill."

You make a gesture like she's being silly.

"No, really. Hollywood actresses live in dog years. Another couple birthdays and I'll be doing *Return of the Leopard People.* They chew you up, then spit you right onto the B-movie casting couch."

"Do you think that was what was bothering her?"

"How do you mean?" says Miss Lupino. She is so much smaller when not projected two stories high.

"Well, apparently she was… well, acting kind of testy. Going after everyone. Like that night at the Trocadero. You were there, correct?" "Absolutely correct. But I think you've got the wrong idea about Clara. It's not like she was on some rampage. In fact, at the beginning of the night she was fine. She was excited about going to London. She's worked films in the UK before, on loan. They love her there."

You ask her about the incidents.

"Well, the one with Mrs. Hale was all Mrs. Hale. She just went at Clara. And I think it's pretty obvious what that was about. But why Camilla chose then and there to confront Clara, I really couldn't tell you. The thing later, though — with Blotto Friedrich and Happy Hughes — that was Clara's doing. I think she'd sunk a few drinks by then. Maybe the stuff with Camilla got her rattled. And then she went for the big boys. It was pretty intense."

You ask what it was about.

"To tell you the truth, I don't really know. Maybe she was sick of running around in the jungle and climbing out of swamps. She used to get good movies, you know? But you do what they tell you. That said, I bet there was more to it than that." She lowers her voice. "Few people know this... but Clara has a sticky past with Otto Friedrich. Something happened between them early in her career. This was before Friedrich ran Orpheum Pictures, when he was just a producer... She never really talks about it. But even from a rough sketch, it looks like Otto was pure sleaze."

"Did you hear what she was saying that night?"

"Something about threats, blackmail, keeping people's secrets... it was veiled but charged, if you know what I mean, with plenty of expletives. Otto was red as a Martian sunset."

"What do you think she was trying to achieve?"

"Ida know." She gives a sudden smile. "My papa used to call me that: Ida Know Lupino. Haven't thought of that in years." She puts down her coffee and stares at the table. "I'm one of the lucky ones. If it weren't for Clara, I'd have fallen in a lot more swamps. But it was like she was finally done with it all — pulling herself out, into a brand new life. Instead, she wound up dead." ◢

Stephen Costa is smooth, and shiny. His tie, the rings on his fingers, the hair on his head — it all has a certain sheen to it. Even his skin looks like buffed mahogany.

"What can I do for you?" he asks.

"The Clara Rose murder," you say.

"Of course, of course." He sits down behind his desk and reaches to a bottom drawer. "Scotch?"

You shake your head. "On duty."

"Of course, of course." He shuts the drawer. "I, too, have much work to do. As you can imagine." He leans toward you across the desk, rings flashing. "A client passing so suddenly — so violently — it makes for really a lot of work."

"How so?" you say. "What could she need from you now?"

"Well…" he leans back, as if happy to have the opportunity to explain. "I have a duty to contact other attorneys about the consequences for their clients in regards to Miss Rose's departure. Most significantly the disposition of the Sidewalk Café. You do know that Miss Rose owned a restaurant…?"

You make a non-commital sort of nod.

"Well technically *part* of restaurant…" continues Costa. "Her silent partner — a man named Ernie Kellogg, will now be sole owner, as per the terms of their agreement." He reaches into the upper drawer this time, and comes out with a *Sidewalk Café* business card. He writes on the back, and slides it across his desk.

"Did you ever get the sense the business was in trouble?"

"You'd be best to talk to her accountant about that. New fellow, by the name of Bob Hall. Shall I write that down as well? Or, of course: you've got your notepad. I should let you do at least something." Costa gives a smooth, shiny grin.

"What happened between her and Fletcher?" you say, purposely switching gears.

"What *didn't* happen?" says Costa, talking with his hands. "Those two were like oil and water — or maybe champagne and moonshine. She'd been trying to divorce him for years — and I'd been trying to help her with that. But it was a complicated set-up; a lot of strings attached."

"But no children."

"No. But a lot of strings nonetheless. And he was a sonofabitch. A mean drunk, and even meaner after the war. Really, though, you should talk to Clara's mother — I just saw her yesterday. She's at Clara's house, right on Fountain and Fairfax, if you want to follow up." ◢

122

You dodge the attack and leap across the bed towards the door, away from your assailant. At least that's the idea. But now somehow he's in front of you — blocking your escape.

You lash out with a quick right jab, but at the same moment, something hits you from behind — lightning flashes through your brain.

You stagger into the corner of the room, trying desperately to find a way to escape. But now you're seeing double: two giant men with flaming hair coming straight at you, pipes in their hands. They swing and connect as the world fades to black. ◢

**In hopes of regaining consciousness,
go to Lead 307.**

145

From afar, Jack Overfield appears over-fed, over-dressed, and nearly over-the-hill. But striding through the parking lot, he's still got a spring in his step. He flicks a half-smoked dart into the air, and holds out his hand to shake. "Can we do this walking?" he says.

You nod, shake, and turn to keep pace. "So you're the producer on *Leopard People*, Mr. Overfield?"

"One of them. And call me Jack."

"Yessir," you say. "Jack. Can you tell me about the shooting?"

"Terrible stuff. Just terrible. Have you talked to Manny Long? He saw more than I did. I did hear the shots though." He makes a gun with his hand: "Boom, then boom." He lights another smoke.

"What can you tell me about Clara Rose?"

"Poor Clara. She could be a real headache sometimes, but deep down she was a great girl. And she had a real spark, both on-screen and off. I truly liked her. Not everyone did, mind you..."

"Why's that?" you say. But the producer's become distracted, calling out to some men with their hands in their pockets:

"Guys, guys, come on! We wrap today. Get the light-stands on the truck!"

You try again: "Who had a problem with Miss Rose?"

"A problem?" Overfield seems surprised. "Oh. Well, our lead actor is a married man. And there was the sense that — well, that neither he nor Clara really respected that. Mrs. Hale just about murdered the girl herself. Called her a harlot, among some more colourful things, in the middle of the Trocadero Nightclub. That could have been a real PR problem, had Clara not died the day after. Now, I'm sorry – you'll have to excuse me…"

And just like that, Overfield is over your questions — striding off to other things. ◢

154

The corridors ring out with the laughs, squeals and shouts of children as you locate Reverend Kurl-Finke, Director of the Jefferson Park Orphanage.

"Come into my office," he says, smiling. "Can't hear yourself think out there."

"Lotta kids."

"City of Angels," says the Reverend. "Now what can I do for you?"

"Clara Rose," you say.

"Ah, that particular angel — gives not just her money, but also her time. And the kids just love her."

You take a breath. "Well. This is going to be very sad news for them. I'm sorry to tell you she's died. Murdered."

The Reverend takes a seat, crosses his chest and whispers a prayer.

"She was one of the truly good ones," he says.

"So she gave a lot to this place? Do you know why?"

The Reverend looks at you. "You're asking why she gave her time and riches to orphaned children? Is that really the greatest mystery?"

"I'm sorry. I suppose not."

"And I suppose there was more to our Clara than met the eye, more than appeared on our screen."

"Of course." You offer your condolences, and walk back through the halls of giggling angels. ◢

222

You find Frank Figone, a cannoli of a man, in the lounge of the administration building, wrestling with a new-fangled coffee machine.

"I hate this stupid beast!" A mix of coffee and cream jets across his security guard's pants.

"Okay," you say, flashing your credentials. "What about the car?"

"What car?"

"Fletcher's. Can you take me to where he parked?"

"He didn't."

"What do you mean?"

"There is no car. At least not on the lot." He manages to maneuver some of the slop into a cup, and starts to slurp. "Could be parked on a street outside the lot."

"Has anyone looked?"

Figone shrugs. "Or maybe he walked? *Slurp.* Took a bus? *Slurp.* Cab…?"

"How 'bout a hot-air balloon?" He stops slurping. "Where were you when the shooting occured?"

"I don't know," Figone takes a smaller sip.

"Is that your official answer?"

"Alright," he says. "I was at craft services. They got *real* coffee there."

If this is who you're relying on to have done a full sweep of the area, you might want to think again. ◢

228

When you turn up at his house, Chaz Borrel is just sitting down to eat. His dining table has a view of his outdoor pool. He doesn't offer you a plate, but seems oddly pleased to see you, gesturing to the seat across from him.

"You don't mind, do you, Detective?" He spreads his napkin on his lap. "Beef bourguignon tastes terrible cold."

You sit down as a woman with a decanter strides from the kitchen and fills Chaz's wine-glass. Her dress and lipstick are ruby red.

"Don't let me stop you," you say.

He swirls the wine, takes a sip, flashes a megawatt smile, and dives into the bourguignon.

"I'm looking into the deaths of Clara Rose and Joe Fletcher. I was hoping to ask a few questions."

"What's to ask about a murder-suicide?" he says, with his mouth full. "Oldest story in the book."

"How are you so certain?"

"Oh, I'm certain of almost nothing, Detective." He points a fork in your direction. "But it does seem a classic equation: Enraged, frequently intoxicated nuisance of a man plus beautiful, wealthy, ex-lover he never deserved. One plus one equals a crying shame. No?"

"Possibly."

He sips. "The ego is a vulnerable thing. Despite all that posturing and talk you see on the silver screen and, well, even right here at this table…" He pats the inlaid mahogany. You notice the bruised knuckles, the crooked nose, the cauliflower ears. One thing's for sure: Borrel is either a boxer or used to be one; you make a mental note to follow up on that one.

"What can you tell me about Thomas Deasy?"

Chaz puts down his fork, picks up the knife, and smiles. "Now that's what you call a case-in-point. Our Tommy could be the poster-boy for *Male Vulnerability*. What do you think: Pay a dime to see that?"

You give a shrug. Chaz stabs a carrot and holds it up to the light. "The thing about Deasy and Fletcher; guys like them: They want to play gangster, they want to play soldier, but they don't want to get too dirty. I can tell you with certainty, because I was a soldier myself - those two boys joined the troops not to fight, but because when all your pals are soldiers you can't just say you're in the pictures and expect to keep getting laid." He snatches the carrot in his teeth, looking at you as he chews. "And even more pathetic, they went to war thinking it'd be like a movie."

"Do you know where Deasy is now?"

Chaz appears to briefly scan his loyalties, then shrugs. "The luxurious Sandman Motel. I think you know it, yes? If you go see Deasy, be sure to let the owner know that the *Sidewalk still has legs.*"

You see a streak of malice cross his gaze.

"Do you know who killed Clara?" you ask.

Borrel seems surprised for a moment, then stabs his food once more.

"You mean other than Joe...?"

You wait.

"Well, I'll tell you. I did hear through the grapevine — something about a red-headed, two-headed monster being hired around town for just this sort of thing..."

"This monster got a name?"

"Got a couple of them, I'd say. But that's pretty much all I'd say."

You're getting tired of Chaz, and your head is throbbing.

"What about you, Mr. Borrel? You got an alibi?"

He puts down the knife, and lets his hands slowly curl into fists, staring you straight in the eye. "Me, I was getting my knuckles painted... Diane!" he calls out to the kitchen, picking up the napkin and dabbing at his mouth. "That was absolutely delicious!"

Then he looks at you as if for the first time. "Oh, I am sorry. I hope you weren't hungry." ◢

232

The woman in the doorway is the spitting image of a once-and-future Clara Rose, had she survived another twenty years. It is like looking at a sad, beautiful ghost.

"Mrs Rose?" you say.

"Ha!" says the woman, "There is no Mrs Rose. Not anymore."

"I'm sorry. I thought you were her mother..."

The woman's eyes flash in anger. "Look, kid, I will always be her mother. But do you really think that was her name? Clara Rose. Heavens to Betsy, people are dumb. That would have worked, too: Betsy Violet. Jennifer Lilly... That's the American dream: a starch-white girl and a pretty flower."

"I'm sorry?"

"You already said that. What exactly are you sorry for? What are you even doing here?"

You explain your position as commissioned private detective. "I'm investigating the death of Clara–"

"Sandy," says her mother.

"I'm sorry?"

"You really gotta cut that from your repertoire. The *sorry* song is flat."

"Sorry." You fumble to take out your notebook. "Is there anything else you can tell me about *Sandy*, that might be of help?"

"You know she had another house, too? She was spending more time there since the break-in. Might be worth knocking on that door?"

"The break-in?"

She looks at you as if trying to ascertain just how much of a clod you really are. "Surely you can talk to the police about that – if you're really commissioned and everything. The officer who caught the kid was a bit of a galoot: Mc-something-or-other..."

"Might you have his card? And also the address of Sandy's other house? Oh, and do you mind if look around?"

She narrows her eyes. "Now you're getting downright pushy." But she shrugs and leaves the door open as she turns. "There's not much to see. We were boxing things up even before it happened — to ship to the new house. Haven't got to the library yet. You can look in there if you want…"

It is a big house, with lots of light, but not as opulent as you might have thought. There are large discolored squares on the wall, where you imagine movie posters might have hung. The library is comparatively small and dishevelled. There's a liquor cabinet with an opened bottle of gin and an empty glass. The desk is cluttered with papers, a vase of wilting lilies, a bottle of diet pills. You find a leaflet for Clara's restaurant, The Sidewalk Café, and jot down the address on Sunset.

You read a few fan letters: A man from Chicago saying he loved her performance in *Two-Eyed Jack.* An orphanage director by the name of Kurl-Finke thanking Clara for another generous donation — and asking when she might be back to see the children. In a drawer, you find a receipt for a *PO Box rental marked #555.* As she reappears you slip the receipt into your pocket, clear your throat and say, " Do you believe it was a murder-suicide?"

She hesitates, then answers: "Murder, yes. Suicide, no. Joe liked himself too much — the kind of troubled that's really only trouble for others. No. Something else must have happened that…" But it catches in her throat — a silent sob. She hands you the information you asked for and turns away. There are two separate address cards — one says *Detective Henry McTeague,* and the other *Clara Rose.* You note the location of the new house, near Gramercy and Olympic.

"Thank you," you say. "I am sorry for your loss."

She looks at you once more, her eyes full of sadness and anger. "Enough with all your sorries," she says. "Go find who killed my baby." ◄

285

Ernie Kellogg has a head like a ball, a body like a pin, and is the sole owner of *Hollywood Bowls! "Ten Lanes of Ten-Pin Stardom!"* Balls thunder down the lanes, making your skull throb. Ernie slurps a malted behind the soda counter, avoiding eye contact with you until the last possible second.

"Get the hell outta here!" he says, with an unsettling grin. "You Agency guys crack me up. Why should I even talk to you?" He takes a long slurp with his straw, gesturing for you to sit down. You get the feeling that mixed messages are kind of Kellogg's forté. And for a silent partner, he's very loud.

"Let me guess? I'm Clara's business partner, so I must have killed her? No, wait — even better: If Clara dies I get a majority stake in the café. And look at that! She died!" The sound of a strike clatters behind you and someone lets out a whoop.

"Majority?" you ask. "Who else has a piece?"

"That scoundrel Tom Deasy. He used to be her agent until he screwed that up. But that's not the point. I'm the one who killed her, right?"

"Uh…"

"Wrong!" he slams the table with the palm of his hand. "You look like a smart kid."

It seems he's expecting an answer to this, staring you down as he takes another sip of his malted. Then he puts up his hand, as if to block what you're going to say. "If you're so smart, then tell me this: Why would I kill her? No really, why? Your reason doesn't make any sense."

You open your mouth. Someone drops a ball.

"Think about it! The Sidewalk Café is Clara's place. And if Clara's dead then what is it?"

You hazard a guess: "Your place?"

"No! What it is, is *not* Clara's place!"

You're about to say you don't follow, but that seems redundant, and there's little doubt in your mind that Kellog is going to explain.

"I'll extrapolate it for you," he says. "I make money when people come to the Sidewalk Café. People come to the Sidewalk Café because it's Clara's place." His face has begun to redden now, from the effort of extrapolating. "I am not a fabulous Hollywood actress, so I *want* it to be Clara's place — *not* Ernie Kellogg's." He is starting to sputter, as if getting lost in his own thoughts. "What is so hard to understand about that?"

You take a moment, hoping he'll remember his malted.

"But isn't it true," you say, as he finally takes a sip. "That even more famous than a movie star is a movie star who's been murdered?"

You're not sure what to be ready for. Though the straw is still in his mouth, you can see the malted sip has halted halfway up. His eyes slowly lift, the sound of a gutter ball echoes in the air. And now his voice comes steady and low.

"Well, that's a very dark thought, my friend. But let's remember: It was yours, not mine."

You nod, and get up to leave, then stop. "Oh, I really should ask you, of course: Where were you when Clara was killed?"

Kellogg smiles and points behind you. "Lane number three. Throwing strikes. Got a half-dozen pinboys for witnesses. Maybe you should have started with that." ◣

291

Your left arm rings out with pain as you block the metal pipe and throw a cross with your right. Your knuckles meet with lips and teeth. But as you're about to bring your knee into things — primarily your attacker's chin — something flashes through your brain: a thudding bolt from the back of your skull.

You reel into the center of the room, trying to find your feet. And now you're seeing double: identical giant men with the same flaming hair, either side of the door, swinging their pipes through the air. ◢

To stand your ground and keep on fighting, go to Lead 307.

To run full speed at the door, go to Lead 614.

293

Glass shudders in the front-door window and your brain rattles in your head, until finally you stop knocking. You step off the porch of the wartime rowhouse. Based on the slats nailed over windows, the general state of the yard, and the fact that nobody's answering, you decide the house is abandoned.

As you're pulling away from the curb, you see a dry-cleaners shop on the corner, a familiar black Chrysler Imperial parked out front. You pull in behind it. The shop sign says *closed*, but then the door is unlocked, so you let yourself in…

"Aha! Finally here to join us!"

The sound and image appear simultaneously: Otto Friedrich's high-pitched voice and his round self, stuffed behind a desk. On either side stands a red-headed giant.

"Come in, come in! There is much to discuss!"

You step cautiously into the light. There is an empty wooden chair with its back to you. The Webb brothers also step forward: identical, except one appears to have split a lip.

"I believe you all have met," says Friedrich. "Which makes *me* the odd man out!" He seems delighted by this turn of phrase, beaming a smile as the twins grab you by the shoulders and force you to take a seat. Your hat falls onto the desk. You barely put up a struggle.

Otto Friedrich gives you a wink, wagging his finger at the ginger behemoths. "Roscoe and Ollie," he says. "In case they skipped that when you met. They can often be perfunctory. But we at the studio would be nowhere without them." Sensing you're here to stay, the brothers unhand you, but you still feel them at your back. You wonder where they keep the pipes.

"It seems," says Friedrich, folding his hands on the desk, "we have many questions to answer. I think we should start with 'Why?'"

"Why?" you say, and feel yourself flinch. You realize part of you is just waiting to be hit.

"Why *you?*" says Friedrich, pointing a finger at your head like a gun. "A movie set? A murder scene? A motel room? My office? Who knows where else? Why always you? It really is very suspicious."

"It… it's my job," you say.

"Ah!" He slams his hand on the desk. "But that just can't be true! And do you know why? Right now we stick with *why?*"

"Why?" you say, flinching again.

"Because it is *my* job! To be on the set. To protect my people — to know where they are, where they were, where they should be. To know what has happened to my actors. To my Clara Rose! And also, of course, to be at my office. *My* job! Not yours!" Friedrich's voice has risen. You can't tell if he's unhinged, or just excited. Blood is thumping against your temples. "So let us try again: The question is *why?* Why *you?*"

"I…" you try again. "I am trying to solve a murder."

"Oh!" Friedrich straightens up. "Is that all?"

You wait. Then nod.

"One little murder? If that is the *What,* it is already solved." He puts his finger-gun between his teeth, pulls the trigger, and laughs. "Simple as an iced lolly, no?" You hear low laughter coming from behind you, too, and shudder.

You take a breath, trying to clear your head. Amid all the menace and bluster, you get a sense of something else, as well — that he truly wants to tell you something.

"Of course you're right," you say, bowing your head just a bit. "I misspoke. It's been a long day. And my head, for some reason, just ain't quite right." You wait. To your ghoulish satisfaction, the Webb brothers laugh again. Then you continue: "Understanding that our jobs are different, yet similar, and there may be more than one murder to solve, and other questions to answer, can I ask one, too?"

Friedrich leans back in his chair. He looks at the ceiling, places his palms on the desk. And then, just like that, the Webb brothers cross back over — into original zoot-suit position. Friedrich looks at you, and nods.

You clear your throat, and go ahead:

"In the middle of the Trocadero, in the center of Hollywood, in front of all the stars, Clara Rose gave her final performance. And by all accounts, it was a doozy: Full of anger and pathos, spit and tears. And of course it was aimed at you. You and Howard Hughes. But I'm willing to bet, mostly you. And I'll also wager that your Clara Rose wasn't acting at all. So I ask you: *Why?*… And I guess also, *What?*"

Otto Friedrich's hands on the desk slowly flex, rising like spiders on their legs. "Alright, then." He looks at you, and smiles. "If you want, I will answer your question. But only with a condition…"

You wait, trying not to glance at the Webbs.

"You," says Otto Friedrich, a spider-leg-finger-gun aimed at your heart, "must promise to believe me."

You look at him, and nod.

"Alright." He seems to settle in, hands becoming human again. "Then I will tell you some things. But it will help to first know this: Nothing I say could possibly harm me. If you are distracted, even for a moment, by such a pursuit, you will sadly miss the points. And then I can't help you at all." He raises a finger and nods, until you nod too.

"Good. The thing to understand is this: There is no difference — no difference at all — between the movies and the mob. They deal in precisely the same wares: violence, sex, escape, impossible dreams, our highest hopes, our basest selves. Both are big business. The biggest. And here, in this town, they are simply one and the same. Together we call them Hollywood. Actors or grifters; agents or soldiers; directors or capos, the studio-head or the big boss — it is all the same play. Except for one thing. And what is that?"

You don't readily know the answer — or where this might be

going. But you flounder around for a guess: "Um. The Academy Awards?"

"Yes!" says Friedrich, to your surprise. "Not just celebrity, or even fame — but actual stardom! It is the exception, and the strongest draw there is: More than money, love or power. And promised to the most random of souls. And here is the thing: If you get close enough, there's no saying what you might let go of, just to try and reach it..." As he says this, you feel a sort of tug — like what he means is almost in your grasp.

"Clara Rose," you ask. "What did she let go of?"

"Well that is the question," says Otto Friedrich. "If you'd asked her — at least that night in the Trocadero — she would have said her soul. And, you see, she believed I took it — oh so many years ago. But, of course, I did not. That's the thing about souls; they're so very small at the start. So easy to lose."

The way he says this, you can't help but see Mephistopheles, sitting right across from you. And somehow you trust his every word.

"But you must have done something. She blamed you for something...?"

"Of course I did something," says Otto Friedrich, mob-boss of the movies. "I let Clara Rose become a star."

"And me. What are you going to do with me?"

"I'm going to let you leave."

The Webb brothers move to where you're sitting, and pull you to your feet.

"But make no mistake," says Otto Friedrich, pointing his thumbnail at your soul, as if ready to gauge it out. "As with Clara, this is not a gift. Not a kindness. It is something to always beware of."

You pick up your hat, look him in the eye, and take your leave. ◢

Perhaps, Agent, it's time to solve the case...?

299

Glass shudders in the front-door window and your brain rattles in your head, until finally you stop knocking. You step off the porch of the wartime rowhouse. Based on the slats nailed over windows, the general state of the yard, and the fact that nobody's answering, you decide the house is abandoned.

As you're pulling away from the curb, you see a dry-cleaners shop on the corner, a familiar black Chrysler Imperial parked out front. You pull in behind it. The shop sign says *closed*, but then the door is unlocked, so you let yourself in…

"Aha! Finally here to join us!"

The sound and image appear simultaneously: Otto Friedrich's high-pitched voice and his round self, stuffed behind a desk. On either side stands a red-headed giant.

"Come in, come in! There is much to discuss!"

You step cautiously into the light. There is an empty wooden chair with its back to you. The Webb brothers also step forward: identical, except one appears to have split a lip.

"I believe you all have met," says Friedrich. "Which makes *me* the odd man out!" He seems delighted by this turn of phrase, beaming a smile as the twins grab you by the shoulders and force you to take a seat. Your hat falls onto the desk. You barely put up a struggle.

Otto Friedrich gives you a wink, wagging his finger at the ginger behemoths. "Roscoe and Ollie," he says. "In case they skipped that when you met. They can often be perfunctory. But we at the studio would be nowhere without them." Sensing you're here to stay, the brothers unhand you, but you still feel them at your back. You wonder where they keep the pipes.

"It seems," says Friedrich, folding his hands on the desk, "we have many questions to answer. I think we should start with 'Why?'"

"Why?" you say, and feel yourself flinch. You realize part of you is just waiting to be hit.

"Why *you?*" says Friedrich, pointing a finger at your head like a gun. "A movie set? A murder scene? A motel room? My office? Who knows where else? Why always you? It really is very suspicious."

"It… it's my job," you say.

"Ah!" He slams his hand on the desk. "But that just can't be true! And do you know why? Right now we stick with *why?*"

"Why?" you say, flinching again.

"Because it is *my* job! To be on the set. To protect my people — to know where they are, where they were, where they should be. To know what has happened to my actors. To my Clara Rose! And also, of course, to be at my office. *My* job! Not yours!" Friedrich's voice has risen. You can't tell if he's unhinged, or just excited. Blood is thumping against your temples. "So let us try again: The question is *why? Why you?*"

"I…" you try again. "I am trying to solve a murder."

"Oh!" Friedrich straightens up. "Is that all?"

You wait. Then nod.

"One little murder? If that is the *What*, it is already solved." He puts his finger-gun between his teeth, pulls the trigger, and laughs. "Simple as an iced lolly, no?" You hear low laughter coming from behind you, too, and shudder.

You take a breath, trying to clear your head. Amid all the menace and bluster, you get a sense of something else, as well — that he truly wants to tell you something.

"Of course you're right," you say, bowing your head just a bit. "I misspoke. It's been a long day. And my head, for some reason, just ain't quite right." You wait. To your ghoulish satisfaction, the Webb brothers laugh again. Then you continue: "Understanding that our jobs are different, yet similar, and there may be more than one murder to solve, and other questions to answer, can I ask one, too?"

Friedrich leans back in his chair. He looks at the ceiling, places his palms on the desk. And then, just like that, the Webb brothers cross back over — into original zoot-suit position. Friedrich looks at you, and nods.

You clear your throat, and go ahead:

"In the middle of the Trocadero, in the center of Hollywood, in front of all the stars, Clara Rose gave her final performance. And by all accounts, it was a doozy: Full of anger and pathos, spit and tears. And of course it was aimed at you. You and Howard Hughes. But I'm willing to bet, mostly you. And I'll also wager that your Clara Rose wasn't acting at all. So I ask you: *Why?*… And I guess also, *What?*"

Otto Friedrich's hands on the desk slowly flex, rising like spiders on their legs. "Alright, then." He looks at you, and smiles. "If you want, I will answer your question. But only with a condition…"

You wait, trying not to glance at the Webbs.

"You," says Otto Friedrich, a spider-leg-finger-gun aimed at your heart, "must promise to believe me."

You look at him, and nod.

"Alright." He seems to settle in, hands becoming human again. "Then I will tell you some things. But it will help to first know this: Nothing I say could possibly harm me. If you are distracted, even for a moment, by such a pursuit, you will sadly miss the points. And then I can't help you at all." He raises a finger and nods, until you nod too.

"Good. The thing to understand is this: There is no difference — no difference at all — between the movies and the mob. They deal in precisely the same wares: violence, sex, escape, impossible dreams, our highest hopes, our basest selves. Both are big business. The biggest. And here, in this town, they are simply one and the same. Together we call them Hollywood. Actors or grifters; agents or soldiers; directors or capos, the studio-head or the big boss — it is all the same play. Except for one thing. And what is that?"

You don't readily know the answer — or where this might be

going. But you flounder around for a guess: "Um. The Academy Awards?"

"Yes!" says Friedrich, to your surprise. "Not just celebrity, or even fame — but actual stardom! It is the exception, and the strongest draw there is: More than money, love or power. And promised to the most random of souls. And here is the thing: If you get close enough, there's no saying what you might let go of, just to try and reach it..." As he says this, you feel a sort of tug — like what he means is almost in your grasp.

"Clara Rose," you ask. "What did she let go of?"

"Well that is the question," says Otto Friedrich. "If you'd asked her — at least that night in the Trocadero — she would have said her soul. And, you see, she believed I took it — oh so many years ago. But, of course, I did not. That's the thing about souls; they're so very small at the start. So easy to lose."

The way he says this, you can't help but see Mephistopheles, sitting right across from you. And somehow you trust his every word.

"But you must have done something. She blamed you for something…?"

"Of course I did something," says Otto Friedrich, mob-boss of the movies. "I let Clara Rose become a star."

"And me. What are you going to do with me?"

"I'm going to let you leave."

The Webb brothers move to where you're sitting, and pull you to your feet.

"But make no mistake," says Otto Friedrich, pointing his thumbnail at your soul, as if ready to gauge it out. "As with Clara, this is not a gift. Not a kindness. It is something to always beware of."

You pick up your hat, look him in the eye, and take your leave. ◢

Perhaps, Agent, it's time to solve the case...?

307

You come to at poolside, face down beneath the *S——-man* sign. Your right arm is dangling into the sludge of the pool. As you pull it out, the toxic stink slides through your bloody nose, into your pounding head.

After a while you manage to sit, then finally arrive at your feet. In the parking lot, you discover your hat, and after that your car. You dig for your keys, but find instead a yellowed piece of paper that you'd shoved into your pocket when the giant attacked. ◢

You open Evidence E.

EVIDENCE
GLOBAL DETECTIVE AGENCY

Location of Collection LOS ANGELES

Sequence No.

E

CERTIFIED COPY OF BIRTH
DEPARTMENT OF PUBLIC

REGISTRATION
DISTRICT No 1923

NAME OF CHILD - FIRST NAME
ANDREW

MIDDLE NAME
ELI

SEX BIRTH DATE
MALE APR. 3, 1930

LEGITIMATE?
NO

PLACE OF
AL

MAIDEN NAME OF MOTHER
MOTHER NOT IDENTIFIED

DATE RECEIVED BY LOCAL REGISTRAR
APR. 5, 1930

This is to certify, that the
appearing on the record of

SIGNATURE OR CERTIFYING OFFICIAL
Archibald R Villey

PLACE OF CERTIFICATION
ALBURQUERQUE, NEW MEXI

STATE OF NEW MEXICO

322

The door to Mrs. Heleker's apartment is only open a crack and all you can see is her husband's eyeball, his chin wagging, and him not being helpful at all.

"I tell you, she ain't here," he says, as a dog barks behind the door.

Then, it seems, the dog gives a pull, and the door swings open wider. And who's standing right behind them but Emma Heleker.

"That's not her!" says the man, regaining his balance.

Emma rolls her eyes, then pats both the dog and the husband on the back as she steps out into the hall. The dog has stopped barking but the man is still sputtering.

"It's okay, honey," she says. "This one's harmless. Isn't even a cop."

"I'm from the Agency," you say, somewhat defensively.

She smiles at you. "Like I said. Come on, let's get some air." She presses the elevator call button, waggles her fingers at her protectors, and steps into the elevator.

As the two of you watch the passing of floors through a steel gate, you glance at her: yellow nails, blue dress, red lips, green eyes, black hair. She takes out a pack of smokes, and one is lit by the time you reach the ground. You step outside together. The clouds in the sky look like giant white fish.

"You want to know about April 2nd, right?" She funnels smoke skyward from the corner of her mouth. "I heard Deasy on the phone with Clara around ten. I could tell she was busting his chops. It wasn't just that he was running a game that night — it was that he hadn't told her."

You ask what Deasy was saying.

"The usual: those hoods are good for business, can't just turn 'em down, yadda-yadda-yadda. When he hung up, you could see him steaming. But he's been steaming a lot lately. Kind of on edge.

He made a couple calls."

You ask who he phoned.

"Not sure, but I think maybe Fletcher. Those two are kind of funny together."

You make some notes, then ask who else was there that night.

"Well Chaz, for sure. He's always around."

"Right," you say. "The famous Mr. Chaz."

Emma laughs, and you look at her with a question.

"People are so dumb. His name is Chaz Borrel. He's just a normal human. But the first time he showed up — this was a long time ago now — someone called him Mr. Borrel, and he said 'No. It's Chaz.'. And I guess he's the kind of goombah that some people take way too seriously, even if they don't know why, 'cuz then they called him 'Mr. Chaz.' And I guess that was fine with him. I mean, what are you going to do? He's the cock of the walk, though. And Deasy's like his little lap dog. I mean, Clara might be his boss on paper, but not in the real world."

You ask about Fletcher.

"Didn't really know him. Just knew *of* him. But I tell you, those guys are all the same: gangsters or wanna-be-gangsters; movie stars or wanna-be-movie stars. They're all just scumbags. The good guys are washing dishes, taking out the trash, maybe trying to solve a murder or two." She winks and blows out an arrow of smoke.

"You like working there?"

"Nope. But somebody's gotta bring home the bacon." She rolls her eyes at the 5th floor window. "And baby always needs that new pair of shoes." She drops the cigarette and stands on it, grinding it under her heel.

You thank her, and watch as she walks back into the building. ◢

335

You arrive at the post office closest to Clara's house and stand in line with a half dozen antsy customers. While waiting for the man in front of you to stop fussing over his stamps, you start to perspire. Finally he's done.

"Next," says the teller.

You smile and nod. "I called ahead from the Global Detective Agency. I'm here to examine a PO Box."

"So what's the number?" ▰

If you do NOT have Clara's PO box number, proceed to Lead 902.

If you HAVE Clara's PO box number and her real surname... add 100 and her surname to the PO Box numberthat number, then proceed to the corresponding Lead.

If you do NOT have Clara's real surname, return to your notes and keep investigating.

404

You'd expect Clara Rose's joint to have a Clara Rose feel to it, or at least a bit of Hollywood glitz, but the Sidewalk Café is remarkably unremarkable. The cozy Tudor-style dining room is empty and the chairs are stacked on tables. But you did walk through an unlocked front door so you figure someone must be here. You stand at the bar, thumbing a stack of menus:

Castellammare Lucullian Dinner, $3.75
Antipasto, Neapolitan or Fruit Cup, Valencia
Coney Island clam chowder or Onion au gratin
Filet of sole, Delmonico or
Baked Virginia sugar-cured ham

"Not open today," says a voice behind you.

A woman in a headscarf has materialized at the foot of a staircase, mop in hand. She scrubs at the floor as you approach.

"I'm not here to eat, though I might come back for the ham," you say, flashing your credentials.

"Oh, the pig is excellent." She glances at your I.D... "I'm Rita. Rita Olsen. The manager of this place. We decided to close, at least for now, with all that's happened. I'm sure you understand. Just keeping busy with some cleaning…" She waves her hand up the stairs.

You tell her you have a few questions, just to confirm Clara's timeline leading up to her death. "Routine follow-ups."

"You'd think it might be part of the police's routine, too. But they haven't asked me anything." She leans her mop on the wainscotting. "Shoot. Wait, don't actually shoot. Do you guys carry guns?"

"Yes," you say. "At least I will, after a probationary period."

"So you're not even a real agent?"

"I'm real. It's just… Can I ask you some questions, Miss Olsen?"

"Shoot," she says again, grinning.

You ask if she saw Clara the night before the murder.

"No. Well, she phoned here to check in. She does that. But what does that have to do with Joe Fletcher? He was banned from this place long ago, before I even started working for Clara, so I wouldn't have seen him. It was him that shot her, right?"

You resist answering, and persist questioning: "So you talked to Clara that night? Were you the only one to speak with her?"

"Well, no. She asked to speak to Thomas Deasy, our bartender. So I put her on."

"What about?"

Rita looks like she's about to say something, but changes tack: "Again, what does this have to do with Clara being shot by her ex-husband? I actually have a lot to do today…" She glances up the stairwell.

"What's up there?" you ask.

"What, upstairs? Just more of the restaurant. More Sidewalk Café!"

"Mind if I take a look?" This time you don't wait for an answer, and she follows you up the stairs.

This might be just more of the Sidewalk Café, but it's also a whole lot ritzier — all chandeliers and velvet rather than stucco and bare beams. Rita is talking quicker now: "This is for our high-end customers. You know — the ones who really want the life that Clara Rose represents. All movie stars and glamor, and, well they want dinner, too, you know, and drinks, and…"

Scanning the room, you see that it's a lot newer than you first realized — the whole building is — probably constructed about thirty years ago, at the start of prohibition… Of course.

"And Seven-Card Stud…?" you say.

"Huh?" You've caught her glancing sidelong at a wall to your right. You walk over and pry at the narrow inlay between two panels, working your arms upwards until at last you feel a latch. You look back at Rita, who says nothing. You find a second latch at the bottom, and the panel slides open, like a diptych in a church. Stored inside are roulette, blackjack, and poker tables.

Miss Rita Olsen is practically vibrating now, unconnected sounds popping out of her mouth. You fix her with a look, and mimic a long, deep breath.

"Relax," you say. "You're not in trouble. At least not yet. Just answer my questions, okay?" She closes her lips, and nods. "The night of the call, there was gambling here. Correct?"

Rita nods again.

"Is that why Clara wanted to speak to Tom? Was he the one letting it happen?"

She nods once more. You make a gesture like it's time to start talking again. She breathes through her nose, and opens her mouth.

"Okay," she says. "Here's the deal. Deasy, Clara and Fletcher all go way back. Tom and Joe are still pals, which Clara doesn't like — I mean didn't like — but they're war buddies, you know; I mean for real, they even fought together. And they both have that gangster inclination, you know, at least since they became civilians again. At first she kind of liked the gambling, thought it was exciting, I think. And Clara always cut Tom a whole lot of slack, but you can see it'd been getting to her lately — the idea that she was losing control of her own place… losing this place to the mob. " Rita looks kind of startled, like she hadn't expected to just lay all this down. You pick up the biggest piece of it:

"The mobsters that come in here. Can you give me some names?"

She looks at you warily, then sighs. "Fact is, I don't even know. Except the big shot of course. But everyone knows him."

You tilt your head and wait.

"Mr. …" she looks around at nothing. "Mr. Chaz."

"That's his name? What kind of name is that?"

"That's what people call him."

You lift up a tarp covering the roulette table. "And he was here the other night? The night in question."

Rita nods. "The games really started heating up. Deasy asked Emma Heleker and Barry Miller to stay and help out. I guess that got back to Clara, and so she was having it out with Deasy on the phone. He was already on thin ice with her, and maybe this was the crack. At least that's what I figure. I try to stay out of all that…"

"That ice…" You slide your hand along the outer wooden roulette rail. "How'd it get so thin?"

"Clara hired a bookkeeper, Bob Hall, and I guess he and Tom were butting heads over inventory. Tom's never been Mr. Reliable, but even more-so lately. Troubles at home, absences, late all the time. I've had to cover the bar a few times. Truth is, he was acting more and more like Fletcher. I could see that sticking in Clara's craw…"

The outer rail is studded with screws. "Have you seen Deasy since the murder?" you say, measuring the space between the screws with your fingertips.

Rita shakes her head.

One of the screws feels loose. You press on it, then again, peering into the ball track of the roulette wheel. A tiny pin emerges, just enough to deflect a ball in its track. You can't help but smirk. "Why, Miss Olsen," you say. "The game is rigged." ◢

444

The waiting area to Otto Friedrich's executive office is festooned with gilt-framed Orpheum movie posters, including Clara Rose's first three box-office hits: *Love Me Sadly, Miss Dakota Pent* and *Shotgun Funeral.* Friedrich's receptionist sits beneath them, unmoved by your requests.

"We're all upset about Clara," she says. "But Mr. Friedrich has already spoken to the police."

You attempt, again, to explain your jurisdiction.

"This is Hollywood," she says, with a tight smile. "The only diction that matters is how you say your lines."

"How about these lines?" you say: "Well-known studio thug, Mr. Friedrich, was one of the last people to see the famous actress alive. In fact, witnesses report that a heated, near-violent, exchange took place between the two of them at the Trocadero Club the night before she was killed. Meanwhile, Mr. Friedrich's receptionist has been charged with obstructing justice."

"Well, would you look at that!" says the receptionist, gesturing to the window. You see Otto Friedrich walking through the parking lot, away from the building, trailed by two redheaded brutes in matching suits. All three climb into a black Chrysler Imperial and drive off. ▰

451

You walk up the front stairs of a grand three-storey house off Pico Boulevard. A tall black woman opens the door before you get a chance to knock. She has smiling lips and crying eyes. You introduce yourself.

"Mae Whitehead," she says. "Clara's things will be picked up tomorrow." She turns back into the house. "I hope whatever you need to do can be finished today."

You follow her into a drawing room with provincial-style furniture. The house hardly looks lived in, and certainly not by Clara Rose. The walls are decorated with Impressionist prints: a sailboat, a flower vase, children playing in the sand.

"She only lived here a few weeks, trying to get away from her troubles. Somewhere further away from that awful man. Look how that turned out." Tears well up in her eyes.

"Would you say you and Clara were close?"

She nods. "She was one of my best friends. I was sad to think of her going abroad, even for a little while. Now she's never coming back."

You can see this is hard for her, but can't tell if she's holding back sobs or something else. You offer a handkerchief from your pocket, and ask if she can tell you more about Clara's plans, as you're trying to establish a timeline. "The night before the murder: She was at the Trocadero. When did she return?"

"Not terribly late, maybe 11:30. A chauffeur dropped her off. She was very upset, crying, but wouldn't tell me what it was about. Oh, Clara…"

"How did she seem the next morning?"

"I couldn't say. She was very quiet. She was going in for reshoots. I think that was the last thing she said. 'We're doing reshoots today.'"

No mention of the night before or even London."

You take a look around the house, but don't find anything of interest. You thank Miss Whitehead for all her help.

"I just hope she's in a better place," she says, and follows you to the door. You hear the radio crackling when you get back to your car. It sounds like the Agency has an update to the case. ◢

To hear the Agency Dispatch
message, proceed to 556.

509

You've finally located the property manager – a squirrely guy named Spiro – among this dingey cluster of bungalow apartments.

"That Fletcher's a boozehound," he says, his knee bouncing up and down behind his desk. "Rather spend his money on hootch than pay what he owes in rent. So I had to kick him out. Why? What's he done?"

"Up and died."

"Holy toledo. What happened? His liver burst?"

"Actually, his head." Spiro winces. You ask him when Fletcher moved out.

"Well I *kicked* him out first of the month. He was eight weeks behind."

"Can I take a look?"

"At an empty bungalow? Sure. You looking for a place?"

You shrug. The manager gets the keys, and you follow him through a courtyard, to Bungalow 18.

"It's cleaned, but not scrubbed down yet," says Spiro, as he opens the door. The air is stale and somewhat pungent. "Comes with its own line, if you want to get a phone. There's even been talk of cable TV. Could be inside a year now. We're pretty state-of-the-art here."

It's small, open-concept – mostly empty but for furniture and appliances. A ceiling fan circles overhead. As Spiro switches it off, the faint odour in the air seems to grow more pronounced. You follow the scent to the kitchen sink, and open the cabinet below. The garbage is full and ripe.

"I can't believe they didn't empty the trash! Going to have a talk with them," says Spiro. You're pretty sure there is no "them". In the bin you find a mostly empty tuna can, coffee grounds, some moldy bread, and a crumpled-up piece of paper. You brush off the coffee grounds and begin to flatten it out. ◢

You open Evidence D.

LAW OFFICES OF

MILLS & COSTA

FAMILY BUILDING

LOS ANGELES, CALIFORNIA

March 29, 1948

Joe Fletcher
5020 San Vicente Blvd
Los Angeles, California

Re: Alimony payments
Effective date: April 1, 1948
Reference: F-0227

Joe Fletcher,

This is notice that the support provisions of the Marriage Separation
Contract (dated February 13, 1946) from Clara Leigh Rose will cease at
the end of this month. The final payment of $150.00 is enclosed with
this letter.

Respectfully,

Stephen Costa
Stephen Costa

Stephen,
There's no way in HELL I'm
done with this you sonofabitch!
Don't think I don't know what's
going on here! I've seen her
with him!

I've been keeping my eyes

543

Two young men in overalls are standing next to one of the Hayes trailers, bickering about how best to maneuver a taxidermied tiger into a delivery van. You ask whose trailer it is.

"That'd be Gwendolyn Tate," says one of them, with a smirk to the other.

You nod a quick thanks, and rap on the door. Then again.

Finally it swings open. A short blonde woman is smiling at you in a way that seems meant to be alluring. She appears both perfectly coiffed and half-undressed.

"Miss Tate?" you say.

"Yes'm." She prolongs the smile. "Are you from the papers?"

"The GDA," you say.

"The Gee-dee what?"

"Global Detective Agency."

"Oh." She lets the smile go and puts her hands on her hips. "Is this about Clara?"

You give a nod.

"Of course it is. Everything is. Whether dead or alive."

"Ma'am?"

"Oh don't ma'am me. I'm no older than you. And I got nothing to say about Clara that you can't go read in the papers. Now if you'll excuse me, I've got work to do."

You don't bother asking what work that is; you just tip your hat as she shuts the door. ◣

556

As you grab some Aspirin from your glovebox, the little red lamp on your two-way radio is glowing red, lighting up your dash like the door of a downtown brothel. You lift the mic and depress the trigger.

"Dispatch," you say. "24 responding from Gramercy Place. Do you copy?"

Miraculously, they do: "Stand by, 24." A moment passes. You chomp on the tablets. "24, we have information on your case. Do you read?"

"Like a book," you say, swallowing the Aspirin dry. "Go ahead."

"Our guys pulled prints off the Clara Rose piece. They also pulled the serial number on your Smith and Wesson: M1917. It's service issue, detective."

"Dispatch, repeat last..."

"Your murder weapon is service issue, detective. But it's not police. The numbers don't match."

"Meaning?"

"Meaning it's got to be military. That's a soldier's gun, Agent."

You squint through the windshield at the sinking sun.

"Roger, dispatch. 24 out." ◢

568

Mrs Hale is clearly not in the mood to talk to you. After what seems like an age standing at her open front door, she finaly takes a breath from her rant; the contents of which centring mainly around *that good for nothing hussy* and *that deadbeat trailer trash husband of hers.*

You take the opportunity, and ask "Can you account for your whereabouts this morning Mrs Hale?"

You're not sure if it is the deep shade of red her face turns or the squeaking noise that escapes her lips, but either way, you can tell she isn't impressed by the insinuation.

"How dare you! Not only was I nowhere near the studio, but I was praying for Clara's soul this morning."

You lean back in your heels, deciding you'll probably learn more if you just let her talk uninteruppted.

She continues, "Clara and I started out together; We read for the same roles, we ended up being cast in the same picture. We were friends, well that was until *Too Give Away A Couple* wrapped shooting. She just took off, without so much as a single word. She was gone for a year or two, I can't remember exactly, but when she came back – she was different. She was move driven than ever. We drifted apart. Sure we were cordial around each other, but something was broken inside her. So broken, infact, that she thought she would try to unroot my life and steal my husband. Not on my watch, I can assure you!"

She is seathing, almost out of breath.

You interject, "So, just to confirm then Mrs Hale, where exactly were you this mor-"

Before you have an opportunity to finished the question the door slams in your face. You tip your hat at the closed door and head back to the car. ◢

571

After finally convincing *Stacy* that the GDA, is infact, a legitimate entity, the travel agent swivels in her chair and starts flicking through a filing cabinet behind her desk.

"Sandy or Sandra, you said?" she asks.

"I'm afraid that's all I have." You say.

"I have three: Sandy M., Sandra C. and Sandra L."

"Have any of them booked a trip recently?"

"All of them, yes." Stacy looks up at you blankly.

"Ok, would you be able to give me their details, *Stacy?*"

"I'm afraid not, we are only permitted to give that information to the *actual* police."

You roll your eyes, "is there anything else you *are* able to share with me *Stacy?*"

"Miss Couples' account is interesting, It looks like we mailed all of the tickets to her. Most of our other travellers pick them up in person." ◢

591

You push through boxwoods and pepper trees, and emerge onto Washington Boulevard.

Beyond the whoosh of four-lane traffic is a gas station. On this side there's only a curb, covered with vagrant grass and scraps of litter. You scan the ground for clues, then see — in the shade of a tree — the reclining figure of a straggly old man.

You approach, and discover that he's not entirely awake — just a little more sleeping-off to do, judging by the Sterno scent and the empty can in his lap.

The truth is, you could also do with a break. This first day on the job is more than you expected. So you sit down next to him, and wait for him to wake...

"Hey, gumshoe," says a voice. "Yer leaning on my tree."

You open your eyes to see that the man is hovering over you now — standing where you were only moments before.

"Got a dime?" he says.

You're about to ask him some questions, but then decide against it. You fish out a quarter and flip it into the air.

Instead of catching it in his hand, he lets it land right in his pocket.

"Neat trick," you say. You turn to leave, then stop. "How did you know I'm a gumshoe…"

"Cuz I was, too," he says. "Before it all went to hell."

As you head back toward your vehicle, the weight of the old man's words lingering in your thoughts. Navigating through the desolate carpark, your tired legs lead you to a shortcut—a makeshift shrub-lined path that separates the less than exclusive VIP section from the crumbing public parking lot.

Lost in your own musings, something catches your eye—an ephemeral glimmer amidst the tangled undergrowth. You crouch down, nestled in the dirt and gravel, partially concealed beneath the foliage, is something unmistakable. You reach into your pocket, retrieving a GDA standard issue evidence bag. ◢

You open Evidence G.

EVIDENCE
GLOBAL DETECTIVE AGENCY
Location of Collection __LOS ANGELES__

Sequence No. _____

Ⓖ

614

You burst through the door into the hazy midnight blue of the Sandman's parking lot. You stumble towards your car, hot blood on your face, the neon buzzing above you. Without looking back at the red-headed demons, you leap into the driver's seat, turn the engine, and peel out onto Robertson Boulevard. Only once your heartbeat has lowered, and you've reached cruising speed, do you take a breath and dig a hand into your pocket. ◢

You open Evidence E.

CERTIFIED COPY OF BIRTH

DEPARTMENT OF PUBLIC

REGISTRATION
District No 1923

NAME OF CHILD - FIRST NAME
ANDREW

MIDDLE NAME
ELI

SEX
MALE

BIRTH DATE
APR. 3, 1930

LEGITIMATE?
NO

PLACE OF
ALI

MAIDEN NAME OF MOTHER
MOTHER NOT IDENTIFIED

DATE RECEIVED BY LOCAL REGISTRAR
APR. 5, 1930

This is to certify, that the
appearing on the record of

SIGNATURE OR CERTIFYING OFFICIAL
Archibald R. Riley

PLACE OF CERTIFICATION
ALBURQUERQUE, NEW MEXI

STATE OF NEW MEXICO

645

Arriving at the LAPD's Robbery Division, you find that Detective McTeague is out on lunch break. You get the sense from his secretary's eye-roll that much of his day is spent in this manner. When he finally shows up, there are three different stains on his shirt.

"What can I do you for?" he asks, offering coffee from a cold pot that you've been staring at for twenty minutes.

"Clara Rose," you say. "And, no, I'm fine."

"That little thing? We picked up the kid who did it. He's back home now. And far as I know the dame ain't pressing, so what's the problem?"

"The dame is dead."

"Uh-oh." He pours himself a cup. "Well, then, you ought to be talking to Homicide." He takes a sip and winces.

You ask if there was anything about the robbery — something that struck him as strange.

"Rich actress getting burgled? Walking target, may she rest in peace."

"So no anomalies?"

"Just the average ones."

"Average anomalies…?" You are starting to lose your patience.

"In these kind of cases the list of things stolen never *exactly* matches the list of things recovered. You give 'em back thirty-three things, and all they do is gripe about number thirty-four."

"Which in this case was?"

"I don't know. Some silver locket. She'll probably find it behind the dresser."

"She's dead."

"Oh yeah. Then I guess she won't."

"What about the kid?"

"Underage. Seventeen, I think he was. Something Needham. Just wanted attention, probably. Or walking-around money. A sniff of her knickers? Maybe all the above…"

"What did he take?"

"Just what it said in the news — a bunch of perfume, some jewellery, trinkets mostly…"

You ask if he can give you an address.

"For the kid? Don't see why, but sure." He pulls open a filing cabinet drawer and starts to flip through folders, spreading one open without removing it from the stack. Then he stops. "Oh."

"Oh?"

"We also found this. Kid said he picked it up in her bedroom. But then she claimed no knowledge." McTeague holds up a piece of paper. "Could count as strange?" ◢

Open Evidence F.

Turn over to next page:

CITY OF LOS ANGELES
CALIFORNIA

ROBBERY
DIVISION

DEPARTMENT OF
POLICE
CITY HALL
LOS ANGELES 12
MICHIGAN 5211

IN REPLYING PLEASE GIVE
OUR REFERENCE

049-1948

INCIDENT REPORT STATEMENT

Det. McTeague

Incident: Burglary

Description of Incident:
At approximately 16:15pm, a burglary occurred a
located at Fountain and Fairfax. The victim rep
arrival, confirmed the theft of several valuable

The following items were recovered and are cur

List of Stolen/Recovered Items:
- 5x Small bottles of various boutique perfum
- 1x Gold necklace. Initials A.E.C.
- 1x Large emerald ring
- 1x Ivory handled hairbrush
- 1x Two-inch .38 Colt Revolver. Initials R.N.
- 4x Various photos of the Actress

Suspect Information:
During the investigation, an underage male
The suspect, identified as Andrew Needham, s
following the incident.

Additional Information:
Upon arrival at the station, Detective Needh
informed the department that the suspect is
the Needham family recently experienced th
contribute to the suspect's erratic behavio

The suspect, Andrew Needham, has been arrested, and the stolen
The motive behind the burglary is still under investigation. The investigation into
the burglary is ongoing as actress has already made contact requesting review of
returned items.

Clara,
I'm begging you for your
own sake! You must stop!
You know you ~~have~~ have
nothing without me! No career,
no cafe, no nothing!
You are mine! And I am
yours! We'll made this
bed and we have to sleep in it.
So come back to bed, Clara.
Before it's too late.
If you leave with him, I'll
kill you both!

657

Of the dozen letters in Clara's post box — most of which look to be fan mail — only two seem of interest; one from the travel agency and a crinkled envelope with no return address. You take out your pocket knife and carefully slice their seals. ◢

You open Evidence B.

0001-21   733900

AMERICAN WORLD AIRWAYS SYSTEM

AIRWAYS, INC.

...ED BY ... AIRWAYS ASSOCIATION

...KET

...ers

Conditions on the next page.

You are forcing us to do this Clara!
Make it easy, and we will go easy on you. Continue to make it difficult, and we will go public!

You can't run away from your past, Clara.
Or from us.

PLEASE PRINT – USE LETRA DE IMPRENTA – PRIME D'ÉCRIRE EN MAJUSCULES

SANDRA COUPLES

NAME – NOMBRE – NOM

LONDON

PERMANENT ADDRESS – COMICILIO – DOMICILE

...NO – ...

...CE/DATE

WORLD'S M...

712

The cracked sign for Bilton Boxing Club buzzes loudly, a dentist's drill of modern lighting, illuminating a stained staircase behind a coin laundry. The doors are pasted with yellowed newspaper and distinctly uninviting. You pop some Aspirin and pull them open.

Inside, a wiry, spectacled man is wrapping a kid's beefy hands in white tape. When he finishes, he holds the kid by the neck and looks him in the eye. "Clean punches, Danny." Danny nods and bounds away.

The man turns, glancing you up and down: "For sure, you ain't a member here."

You ask about Chaz Borrel, and if he was here on the day Clara was killed.

"Mr. Borrel, you say?" The gym goes quiet. A crowd of large men drifts towards you... "He was here Saturday morning, after church of course. Sparred with Little Bruno over there." He points over his shoulder. The heavyweight encroaching on your personal space forces you to step around him.

Little Bruno claps his chalky hands together, making clouds in the air like some vengeful thunder god. He digs the balls of his feet into the concrete beneath an impossibly loaded barbell, grabs hold with a wide grip…

"Excuse me," you say.

Bruno lets out a defeated sigh.

"Do you spar with Chaz Borrel?"

He sidesteps the bar, scooping more chalk from a bucket, thousand-yard stare sizing you up. "Who wants to know?" he says. At least that's what it sounds like. You can barely hear him over the speed-bags and fans.

"I'm with the Global Detective Agency. Can you tell me when

you saw him last?"

Little Bruno motions for you to come closer. When he whispers in your ear, you realize there's something wrong with his voice. It's like he's been punched in the throat. "Saturday," Bruno forces, rubbing his chalked-up hands. "Every Saturday. After church."

"Thanks, big guy," you say.

He winces a smile, claps his hands in the air, and steps to the bar again. ◢

789

William Hale is wearing a silk leopard-print bathrobe, and holding a tumbler of whisky. Even for a movie star, his face is disturbingly symmetrical. The effect is even more pronounced when reflected in the make-up mirrors.

"I hope you don't mind if Miss Andrews here strips the old mug while we talk." He gives you a puzzling wink. "It's been a helluva day."

Miss Andrews, a tiny woman in a checkered dress, nods demurely and starts dabbing Hale's cheeks with a sponge.

"I wish I had more to tell you." He swirls the rocks in his glass. "Honestly, I do. I'm here in this trailer, doing my vocal warm-ups, and the next thing I know, Clara is… gone." He lowers his already deep voice, holding your eyes in the mirror. "It baffles the mind, how quickly a light is snuffed out."

"How would you describe your relationship with Miss Rose?"

Hale glances at Miss Andrews, who has removed a layer of thick black makeup from one of his eyebrows, but not the other. She avoids his gaze.

"Clara and I were lovers," he says, as if narrating an opening scene. "Nothing to be ashamed of; we're all adults here. We had chemistry, undeniable chemistry. We were magnetic together on screen – and off-screen, fireworks! Of course, we weren't exactly a couple. I'm married, after all."

"And so was she, no?"

"On paper, I guess. What a waste!"

You close up your notebook. "That's some robe."

"*Leopard People,* leopard print… The crew gets a real kick out of it." He winks again. Then a thought streaks across his perfectly proportioned face… "Oh hellfire! What's going to happen to production?" He looks at Miss Andrews. She looks away. You exit the trailer. ◢

810

If you haven't met Dimitri before, then you should find somewhere else to be.

"Um," says Dimitri, tentatively. "Again with you? Do you have no things better than to bug-up my guests?"

You give him a don't-mess-with-me look. Apparently the day's been so long you've already acquired some gravitas — or maybe it's just the bruises. He begrudgingly fetches the register, and keeps glancing at your face as you scan the pages.

And there it is, four rooms down from C.Gable: *J.Cagney*. What a couple of cut-ups. You write down the room number.

Dimitri suddenly grabs your wrist with surprising strength.

"I've been instructed to not let anyone see Mr. Cagney without the secret phrase."

You pull free of Dimitri's grip, and remember: something about sidewalks and legs... ◢

Do you know the secret phrase?

If so, subtract 199 from the Lead where you got it, then go to the new one.

824

Your buddy Ray, who parks cars at the Wilshire Country Club, gives you a call when Howard Hughes tees off. Then, for a couple of dollars more, he looks the other way as you slip past the gate and head towards the fourth hole.

A tall, familiar-looking man in a yellow shirt and khakis is waggling a five-wood, peering at the horizon. Someone grabs your shoulder from behind. You turn to face two goons in Hawaiian shirts — one of them holding a finger to his lips, the other one tapping the holster under his arm. The three of you watch silently as Howard Hughes strikes his ball. It hooks into the fescue.

"Look what you made him do," says the man still gripping your shoulder. Hughes is striding down the center of the fairway.

"My apologies," you say. "I just need a moment of his time."

"You and everyone else," says the one with the holster. "Mr. Hughes don't like to be bothered." The two of them grab your arms and walk you back to the fourth tee, then the first, then all the way to the parking lot. Ray is studying his shoelaces as they send you on your way, with a little extra push. ◢

834

When you arrive at Thomas Deasy's house, there is a white Chevrolet in the driveway, but nobody answers the doorbell. You go around back, where you find a woman on her knees in the garden, hair tied up with a colorful scarf. She gives you a quick glance. "If you're looking for Tom, I kicked him out." She stabs her trowel into the earth, carving out a heart-size hole.

You introduce yourself, but she doesn't seem interested. She sinks a white rose into the hole and digs her fingers through the soil around it. Apparently satisfied, she stands up and removes her gloves.

"I'm Samantha," she says, "and Tom is a cheating scumbag. I'm not sure what else there is to know."

"Do you know where he is?" you ask.

"Don't know and don't care. Out every night, gets home smelling of cigars and women."

She walks towards the house. You follow her into a crowded back entry filled with gardening supplies. She moves some empty pots to retrieve a bag of fertilizer, hands it to you and plants her hands on her hips.

"Say, you want a drink?"

"I can't," you say. "On duty. But thanks."

You carry the fertilizer out and set it down on the grass. Then you leave Samantha Deasy your card, in case her husband turns up. ◢

864

You are at the home office of Bob Hall, accountant.

"Well, I wasn't officially her accountant," he says. "Miss Rose hired me as an auditor, on an informal basis."

You take a sip of the ice water he's poured for you, and ask what that means.

Hall sits down behind his desk, his back perfectly straight — as is the ledger on the desk, the pencil next to it, the part in his silver hair, his pocket square and bowtie… "It means that I was asked, by her, to check the books for irregularities."

"And did you find any?"

"That, I did."

"Can you tell me about them?"

"That, I can."

Hall walks to a filing case, retrieves a small file and places it precisely in the center of the desk, squaring the edges as he opens it. "The records are quite thorough for hash-house standards. And all the money that left her café made it to the bank. But that's where the good news ends."

"So what about the bad?"

Hall draws four sheets from the file, and spreads them evenly across the desk. There is more red than white or black. You squint through the slaughter. "What am I looking at?" you ask.

"Each loss is marked in red," he slides a finger down a column, "A dollar here, a dollar there doesn't look like much. But in aggregate," his finger stops at a five-digit number in the negative. "Some of it's damaged inventory, some is 'no-sales' on the register tape, then there is labor where what's been paid is double or triple over labor hired.…"

"Okay," you say. "So maybe Clara and her friends aren't the best businessmen? Maybe it's more about the generosity — free drinks, parties, torn-up dinner bills… After all, her main job was being a movie star, no?"

"This kind of generosity," says Hall, tapping the file for emphasis, "you don't recover from."

"Long and short of it?"

"My professional opinion? Someone was bleeding the café dry. Someone other than Clara Rose."

"The silent partner?"

"Ernie Kellogg? There's a chance he knew. But all signs point to Thomas Deasy. And you've got to understand, Clara Rose wasn't just doing this for fun, this represented the next stage of life for her — a secure future after the movies."

"Did you get a chance to tell her."

"I sure did," says Hall, with something like regret in his voice. He touches the ink-strewn paper. "And the next thing I know, she's the one covered in red." ◢

866

As you walk along the cattle fence bordering the northern edge of the studio lot, the ground beneath your feet crunches with each step. You look down and notice the scattered fragments of broken glass across the dirt path. ◢

888

You recognize her from the movies: always the heroine's sister, or the detective's receptionist, or the chatty waitress in a diner... But today Alice Doone, sitting in her trailer, looks like someone who's just lost a friend.

You clear your throat, and take out your notepad. "Can you tell me about the last time you saw Clara?"

She's looking down at her own hands in her lap, like they're a couple of birds dead in a nest.

You try again: "You saw her just before it happened, no?"

Doone nods, and now she looks up. Her eyes are like strawberry moons, red and distant. "I wanted to talk to her — see how she was doing after last night. But she acted like she didn't have time."

"Anything else?"

"Her Director was looking for her, like usual. I told him which way she went. It was barely a minute later that I heard the shots."

"Can you describe them?"

"Bang, bang." She picks up a tissue and dabs at her eyes. "Then I saw Hale."

"Who?"

"William Hale…? Movie Star? Ladies man? Talk of the town? I told him it was gunshots. And he just went white and flighty as a pelican — wouldn't even come with me to check it out. Some hero."

You ask her about finding the body.

"It was like I just knew... I knew everything that had happened, and just how awful it was. I knew she was dead. I knew Joe shot her. And I'll tell you what: I wished he was still alive so I could shoot him myself. But you know what else?"

You say you don't.

"It wasn't just Joe who killed her. It was all of them. It was this whole damn town." Alice Doone begins to sob. "Oh my God. I'm going to miss her so much." ◗

902

"Sorry, I think you have the wrong post office," says the teller, snapping her gum as she looks through the register. "We don't have that P.O. box, *or* that name... Hey, isn't she some movie star?"

You thank her, and head for the door. ◢

905

If you have found Deasy, come on in.

If not, what are you still doing on the lot?! Get back out there.

Miss Andrews sits in the corner of the trailer organising a menagerie of wigs, prosthetic noses and, what look like, animal teeth – she barely looks up as you enter.

"Miss Andrews, do you mind if I borrow a moment of your time?"

You gear up for your full introduction as she turns around to look at you. But instead of hearing you out she raises her voice over yours, "Sure, but I'm not sure I'll be able to help."

You stand at the doorway like a dear in headlights as she gestures to a lone chair at the far end of the trailer.

"Anything you can share with me may help, Miss Andrews."

She nods as she turns her attention back to the table of equipment.

"You must spend a lot of time with the actors before and after shooting, did anything seem strange this week on set?"

"Not really, I was assigned to Mr Hale for the entirety of this production, so apart from his usual sneaking around, nothing out of the ordinary."

"*Usual sneaking around?*" you ask.

"Nothing revelatory, it is common knowledge that he and Clara were having an affair. Poor Mr Hale didn't know what hit him, he was just one in a long string of relationships for her."

"What do you mean," you press.

"*I mean*, Clara got what she wanted. Mr Hale wasn't the first man on the lot she had stuck her claws into. Funnily enough, it was the men she brought in from the outside that drew the most attention."

"The outside? You mean she was able to bring in people who didn't work for the studio?"

"Exactly, it was all Mr Hale talked about this week – the young man she had brought in to replace him. He knew their relationship was over, so he was scrambling to repair things with his wife."

You sit there processing. Penny clears her throat and points a hand in the general direction of the door. "Now please, if that is all, I'm trying to get ready for the next scene."

As you reach the door, you think about asking her about the nature of her relationship with Deasy, but you get the impression that won't go down so well. Instead, you tip your hat and thank Miss Andrews for her time. ◢

912

**If you have been here before,
with a motel room key in your hand,
go to 810.**

**If it's the first time you've been here, and you
don't have a key, you should go and find one.**

**If you've got a key,
Welcome to the Sandman!**

In a city of scuzzy flophouses, this one is something else. The "a-n-d" is burnt out over the boulevard, so that the giant buzzing sign reads The *S——-man Motel.* Somehow the air in the parking lot is twice as humid as the rest of L.A.

As you lock your car door you can hear something bubbling from the swamp that once might have been the swimming pool. The front office has an Armageddon sort of charm, and a gaunt man behind a desk appears to be hunting cockroaches with a charged, frayed electrical wire.

A magnetic nameplate on the counter reads: *"DIMITR is happy to help."*

"Dimitr?" you say.

"Dimitri!" barks the man, tiny forks of lightning flashing on his desk. "Package only come with two i's."

"Dimitri," you say.

"You want room?" A charred roach goes flicking off the desk.

"That I do." You pull out the key from your pocket. "I'll need to take a look at number three. But first, can you tell me who's renting it?"

"Psha! Take hike instead!"

"Well that's not very helpful, Dimitri." You take out your GDA badge and put it on the counter. "You can either give me your registry, or that phone on your desk — and we'll call my colleagues at pest control. Also building inspection. Maybe IRS while we're at it…"

"Psha!" he says again, but drops the wire and picks up the registry. "Room Three…" he says, opening the binder on the counter and putting his finger on the page: "Mr. C. Gable."

"You're kidding, right?" You put the key on the counter and turn the book around. Dimitri is not, in fact, kidding… "That's it? That's all the information you've got?"

He shrugs. "Why I not trust my guests?"

"Well, let's go take a look." You pocket your badge, and pick up the key.

When you arrive at the room, you find that the key is redundant; door number 3 is already open. The wood around the lock has been splintered. You turn to confront Dimitri, but he's disappeared. Pushing the door wider, you step inside.

The room is dark. You run your hand along the wall by the door, looking for a lightswitch, but find nothing. As your eyes adjust, you see the shape of a double-bed, lamps on either side, and you go to turn one on, fumbling beneath the shade.

The room fills with an orange glow. There is a dishevelment of bedding and clothes, and there, on the bedside table, a yellowed piece of paper. Picking it up, you hear a movement behind you.

You turn fast, as a shadow becomes a shape, becomes the figure of a man: a very large man with orange hair in the orange light. There's something in his hand. As he swings for you, you pocket the paper, and duck. The lamp crashes to the floor but the bulb is intact, casting shadows across the ceiling. The man swings again. ◢

Evade the attack, and bolt for the door? Go to Lead 122.

Block the attack, and fight back? Go to Lead 291.

915

Passing through a hedgerow bordering Orpheum Pictures, you emerge on to Washington Boulevard. A tumbleweed blows across the street as you walk towards the lone car parked in front a gas-station: a Chrysler Town and Country convertible. The doors are locked.

You try the keys you found in Fletcher's pocket, opening the door on the first try. Surveying the interior of the car, you climb into the driver's seat. It's comfortable: not this year's model, but you can still smell the leather. You lean over and pop the glove box. ◢

Open Evidence C:

997

You stride through Rathbuns grand entrance and are immediately
struck by an intense waft of bergamot and lemon. The room not
only smells expensive, but it looks expensive; the store is adorned
top to bottom with all manner of exotic looking garments, draped
over snooty-looking mannequins, all presided over, by an equally
snooty-looking woman. As you approach the register, a heavy sneer
cast across her face betrays how impressed she is with your arrival.

"Can I help you?" she offers, looking down her nose at you.

"I'm with the GDA, investigating a murder," you respond calmly.

"I'm not sure what help you think I will be, but I can assure you,
I would prefer to be kept out of any murder investigation, and so
would our discerning clientele," she says dismissively, with more
than a hint of disdain in her voice.

"Of course," you say, "I won't be long, I'm trying to find an *Emerald
Green* dress – more specifically – the individual who purchased it."

She rolls her eyes and casts a sarcastic look around the store.
"Do you have any idea how many garments we sell in a single day?
Look around you. It will be exceedingly difficult to provide you with
information, if any at all."

"The dress was worn by Mr-" you begin.

She violently gestures for you to lower your voice, "Please, our
client's rely on us for our discretion and annonymity." She hisses
at you.

"The dress was worn by a certain handsome actor's wife," you
explain, whispering each word. "Someone who, from what I've been
told, has a strong opinion and isn't afraid to express it."

The cashier studies you for a moment, assessing her options.
Deciding it would be better just to get you our of the store, she leans
in close, "If I give you an address, will you please leave us in peace?"

"Most certainly," you say with a charming smile.

She scribbles down an address on a scrap of paper and hands it to you, before shooing you away with a dismissive wave. You take the paper and as you leave, you unfold it. Before you is what looks to be a rough sketch of a street corner somewhere, the letters H and 3 underlined. ◢

READY TO SOLVE THE CASE?

If you are, please turn the page and answer the questions listed in **FINAL REPORT 15a.**

Have you written out your answers?

If you are ready to reveal the truth,
please turn over to next page:

SOLUTION

FINAL REPORT 15a

Who killed Clara Rose?

....

....

Who killed Joe Fletcher?

....

Who was sending threatening letters
to Clara?

....

What happened on April 3, 1930?
And how do you know?

....

....

....

Who were you attacked by, and where?

....

....

....

SOLUTION

You ask him to continue.

"I don't know. I thought he was going to keep on shooting. I grabbed my dad's gun from under my shirt and ran at him, but even as we fought, I knew my mom was dead. Both of my moms. And I think I was screaming. I fell back, and the gun was pointing up at him. He leapt onto me, and I pulled the trigger."

Andy is shaking now, staring at the locket in his hands. You stand up, and slowly walk with his father across the yard, out of the boy's earshot.

"That's it," says Ex-Detective Needham. His voice is sad, tired, but resilient.

"Yeah," you say. "I guess that's it."

"Looks like Fletcher shot himself after all," he stops walking and turns to you. "Don't you think?"

You look back at Andy — such a singular boy of a man, sitting beneath the banyan tree. You didn't sign up for this, couldn't expect it, and sure as hell don't need it.

You turn to his father, look him in the eyes, and nod.

THE END.

"Then in one moment it all just changed. Joe Fletcher moved towards us — like he was going to hug us, or hit us, I don't know. But my mom, Clara, just started yelling — for him to get away. To get away from us. Then Joe was yelling too. Or more like growling."

You ask what Fletcher said.

"I'm the one who gave it to you! I thought he meant the locket, but then he was looking at me. And that's when he started with the question. He called it 'Otto's question'. Kept yelling. 'Tell him the question! At least tell him the question!' Andy is getting more distraught. You ask him to take a deep breath. He does. Then you ask about Otto's question. He breathes again, and again. His eyes go steely:

"You have to decide, Clara Rose!"

Andy rises to his feet. His voice is booming, his nostrils flaring, like he is channeling Joe Fletcher quoting Otto Friedrich. For a moment you see his mother's stage presence, her talent:

"You have to decide, Clara Rose! It's really very simple: Are you a mother... or are you a movie star?" And just like that, the breath goes out of him. He sits back down at the table, closes the locket. You ask what happened next.

"She... She started to laugh. And I remember just what she said. She said, 'That's not the question, Joe Fletcher, is this: Are you still so dumb, after all these years, that you really think he's yours?'" Andy's intonation is impeccable. It's like his mother is there, mocking you all beneath the banyan.

You ask what happened then. Andy looks at you:

"It was madness. She was laughing and crying all at once, like she was trying to sing. And then — just like that — the whole world exploded."

You ask him to explain, to slow it down.

"I don't know. I saw the gun. It was in Joe's hand. His eyes were glowing red. Fire leapt out of the gun. And my mother flew against me. She hit me like a falling tree and crashed onto the ground."

up at my school — said he'd written that letter. He showed me my... my bir-th-certificate. Told me he was my dad. He said my mother was in danger, and we had to help her. I didn't know what to do. I know I should have told my dad — *I mean my real dad.*"

Andy looks at Reggie Needham.

"But I didn't. I wished my mom was still alive. I mean my mom-mom, not my birth-mom. She died two years ago."

He looks at the locket on the table.

"I guess I got kind of obsessed with seeing my mom. I mean Clara Rose. I watched all of her movies, again and again. And I tried to find her house. I just really wanted to see her. And protect her. Of course she wasn't home, but I did find a letter, and I knew at once it was from my birth-dad. It had the same handwriting as the letter he'd sent me. And that's when I knew. He was the one who was threatening her, trying to hurt her. I also found that..." He points to the locket. You ask him to continue, to proceed to the day of the murder.

"It was the day after they let me out. He came to my school. Said we were going to see Mom, for my 18th birthday. I was both excited to see her and frightened as heck. I knew I had to try and protect her, to help her, to save her..."

Andy starts to cry. Then chokes it down and continues:

"At first it was like a dream — like an actual dream I had. There was a cannon there, a noose, and both of my birth parents. My heart was pounding so hard I could hear it. My mom was more beautiful than I ever imagined, and she was right there. At first she looked shocked, then worried. But then she just smiled at me. And it was like everything was going to be okay, no matter what. I had a mom..."

Andy is crying now, but continues his story:

"I... I had the locket. I just wanted to give it to her — to give it back to her. I felt her hands. That was the first time I ever touched her — I mean, that I remember. And she was holding the locket, and smiling at me, and crying. Smiling right at me. She kept saying we were going to go away. Start the life we never had together..."

He grabs the locket off the table, and looks at you:

Turn the page to continue.

Start Here.

When you arrive, Officer Hickman, Detective McTeague and a couple of stern looking beat cops are already assembled in front of the house. No one looks out for their own like the LAPD.

You nod, say good day, and make your way up the front stairs — with only a bit of elbow jostling. You can't help but admire the loyalty — or at least the show of it. The arrest warrant would have easily leaked, but you doubt they know much more than that.

You knock on the door, and it opens. Ex-Detective Reggie Needham looks you in the eye, and for a moment you're unsure — not of the case, no longer of the case — but of what he's going to do. He stands aside, and lets you in.

"Where is he?" you ask.

Needham takes a moment, then a deep breath. *"Backyard,"* he says. And together you walk through the house.

At a rough-hewn, hand-made picnic table, in the shade of a banyan tree, sits young Andy Needham, born Andrew Eli Couples. His father walks towards him, and it's only now you see how different they look, though in so many ways they seem so alike.

You take out the locket, open it up, and put it on the table. Clara Rose at 18 years old, when she shot her first movie: To Give Away a Couple.

Andy looks at you, and you can see his mother's eyes, full of pain and regret.

"Do you have anything to say for yourself, Andy?" you ask. With his head in his hands, he begins his confession:

"I knew I was adopted. My parents told me. And I really was okay with it. But then, about a year ago, I got a letter in the mail, telling me who my birth-mom was.

"I thought it might be a joke, but it kept digging at me. Then a man showed

CLASSIFIED DIRECTORY

- OF THE CITY OF -

LOS ANGELES
CALIFORNIA

- FOR THE YEAR -

1948

-
Business Firms
Agencies
Residents
-

Informants

You have insiders that are always available to offer insight or advice that can help you with your investigation.

Ella Crane
Agency Supervisor (O10) at M4.
Your supervisor.

Nolan Graves
Coroner (O11) at J4
You're friendly with the coroner who can help you interpret the cause of death of autopsy information.

Trudy Stein
Agency Archive & Records (O12) at M4
The Agency has a private collections library that can help you with historical information and public records.

Feswick F
Your Agency Colleague (O13) at M4
Experienced Agency operative. You sit next to him.

Agnes Ross
Newspaper City Editor (O14) at L3
Editor at the Los Angeles Examiner.

Joe Muggie
Taxi Driver (O15) at L4
He knows a lot. Sometimes it's even useful.

Edie Elan
Hollywood gossip columnist (O16) at 21
Edie Elam is terrifying to actors and a good source on the movie business.

Carl Burlage
Police informant (O17) at N4
An honest "square apple" within the LAPD.

Cecil Neddie
Underworld informant (O18) at 21
He likes to remind you he's not a snitch!

BUSINESS DIRECTORY

ACADEMIC

Glendale Ac. of Beauty Culture 818 (L4)
Monticello School for Girls 596 (E4)
St John's Academy.......................233 (P4)
St Vincent's School 953 (J4)

ACCOUNTING SERVICES

Leslie Accounting........................001 (F4)

ADMINISTRATIVE & SPECIALTY SERVICES

County Morgue............................011 (J4)
Global Detective Agency HQ 010 (M4)
James H B Detective Serv 309 (R3)
Jameson Petroleum Co 417 (I3)
St Helen's Petroleum Co Ltd 395 (N4)

ALCOHOL & BEER

Glenbrae Distilleries Ltd 849 (P2)

ALTERATIONS & SERVICES

Avon Clnrs & Dyers......................199 (N4)
Baby Diaper Services 745 (R2)
Baby Garments Serv 532 (A5)
Baby Laundry Serv.......................201 (Q4)
Boston Clnrs & Dyers 371 (C5)
Boston Modern B. & B. Mfg Co......605 (K5)
Cevola Shoe Reprng Shop..............204 (N4)
Dress Code Authority....................221 (L4)
Glen Alva Cleaners.......................882 (E5)
Glen-Jackson Clnrs.......................500 (I1)
Pauline Garment Mfg Co 595 (D2)
St Regis Cleaners & Dyers..............095 (L3)
Swan Dry Clnrs 448 (E2)

APARTMENTS

Babette Apts..............................065 (P2)
Chalet Apts................................586 (R3)
Deodar Apts...............................264 (Q5)
Drexel Apts................................381 (L5)
Glen Abbey Apts 836 (C6)
Gleasner-Fraizer & Dunn Rl Est 633 (D4)
Monticello Apts...........................298 (F5)
Montrose Apts.............................756 (N3)
Paulsen Apts 376 (D3)
St Johns Apts 163 (F4)
St James Apt..............................566 (G4)

St Lawrence Apts.........................604 (F3)
St Leger Apts 749 (O5)
St Regis Apts 896 (L4)
Woodford Arms Apartments 809 (E5)

AUTO NEW & USED DEALERS

Chaffey Ned Autos 473 (J6)
Ford Motors...............................338 (D5)
Statler Studebaker 896 (L5)

AUTO SERVICES PARTS & SUPPLIES

Aye and Stearns Inc. 554 (H3)
Bose Charlie Auto Tire Shop 767 (P1)
Bosch-Zenith Sales & Serv Co 495 (L4)
Boston Auto Salvage.....................979 (H3)
Chaffee's Garage 406 (B2)
De Paolo Motor Serv.....................077 (R5)
Dresover Lip-Shield Co...................642 (Q2)
Ratkowski G E Auto Serv 915 (D6)
St Paul Garage 549 (Q4)
Saitman's Brake Serv Co 933 (H4)

BARBERS & BEAUTY SALONS

Avocado Beauty Shop....................970 (M2)
Dressen's Barber & Beauty Shop ... 619 (F4)
Glave Oil Permanent Wave Shop...718 (H6)
Glen Arden Beauty Serv.................800 (R2)
Kelsey's Beauty Shoppe 779 (D2)
Paule's Beauty Salon 449 (G3)
Pauline's Bleach & Dye Studio.........143 (G6)
Woodcrest Beauty Salon 063 (M4)

CLOTHING

Baby Accessories Co 085 (A5)
Baby-Aide Products Inc 448 (R3)
Baby Equip Co 342 (C6)
Baby Scale Rental Serv Co..............858 (J3)
Baby Shop..................................405 (M4)
Chaikin Bros Fur Co 257 (H3)
Chain Belt Co 423 (F5)
Denwitt Lingerie Shop....................062 (M3)
Denslow's Sport Shoppe 830 (L4)
Moody Bros Diamond Setters.........755 (O6)
Paulson's Store 370 (D4)
Rathbuns Dept Store......................997 (Q1)
St Paul's Misfit Clothing Co 297 (B2)

BUSINESS DIRECTORY

COMMUNITY ORGANIZATIONS

Avoy Social Club.............................263 (G2)
Axelros & Sons Monuments...........627 (B6)
Bosserman & Warren Mortuary 249 (E5)
Jefferson Park Orphanage..............154 (H6)
Moon Theatre.................................736 (D5)
St John's Catholic Church..............273 (J6)
St Vincent's Church 302 (R3)
St Joseph's Church 460 (C2)
St Paul's Presbyterian Church........328 (N1)
St Philip Community Center...........741 (M3)
St Stephen's Episcopal Church 607 (C4)
St Thomas Episcopal Church.........960 (O3)
Woodlawn Cemetary 497 (P4)

CONTRACTOR SERVICES

Chaffin Ethel Painter......................821 (L4)
Dri Seal Co Paint 200 (O1)
Jameson Lock & L. Mower Shop....993 (Q2)

DENTISTS

Boston Smile Co.............................238 (O3)
Swan Vernon R Dntst......................203 (O3)
Weld E L Dntst 802 (B5)

EMPLOYMENT & CAREER RESOURCES

Boston Employment Agcy..............661 (I2)

ENERGY & POWER

Bachman Distrbng Corp.................160 (F3)
Glen-Airy Distrbng Serv Co............606 (P6)

FURNITURE

Baby Line Furn Co..........................730 (F1)
Babylon Lamp & Shade Co 989 (J3)
Bosley Furn & Trans 274 (M4)
Boston Bedding Co 153 (N5)
Denver Trans Van & Stge Co 447 (K4)
Moody A & Co Inc mattresses 799 (R3)
Rath Packing Co.............................964 (C2)
The Chair Factory 488 (F2)
Woodcraft Table Co 131 (E5)

GROCERY

Boston Kosher Meat Mkt.................704 (L5)
Ceylon Tea & Coffee Co 350 (I2)

Denver Grocery..............................924 (N3)
Drexel Grocery & Meats Mkt.........227 (I4)
Dried Food Products Co Ltd 128 (C5)
Glazelnut Donut Co 284 (Q6)
Glen Airy Public Mkt......................681 (G4)
Moon Fish Co 196 (G6)
Welcome Market............................403 (O5)
Welch's Candy Co 432 (B5)
Woodcrest Public Mkt 118 (E3)
Woodman Bros Day & Nite Mkt....181 (F6)

HARDWARE SUPPLIES

Bosch Amer Sales & Serv Co A. 474 (C3)
Bostitch Sales & Serv Agcy.............332 (C5)
Denny and Miller Engnr..................361 (Q3)
Slade F M Lumber 559 (A3)
St John A S Explosives....................256 (F2)
St Louis Fire Brick and Clay Co 567 (J3)

INSURANCE

Boston Ins Co Marine Dept.............148 (M5)
Rathbone King & Seeley Inc 830 (I3)

LEGAL

Barnett & Robertson.......................038 (N8)
Clendenen Legal............................055 (H1)
Gleason's Attorney Serv Co 333 (F4)
Mills & Costa.................................117 (P4)
Raunch L C & Associates................097 (L5)

LODGING

Avon Hotel 773 (A3)
Biltmore Hotel 066 (E4)
Chalfonte Hotel 369 (G2)
Deodar Inn 268 (J2)
Elmar Hotel 777 (N6)
Figueroa Hotel 021 (F9)
Flamingo Hotel 099 (F4)
Imperial Hotel 111 (M4)
Liberty Hotel 977 (E4)
Paula Hotel 563 (F1)
Sandman Motel 912 (D3)
St Paul Hotel 159 (F3)
St James Hotel 348 (G5)
St Vincent's Maternity Home..........521 (C4)
Sunrise Motel 112 (D5)
Viceroy Hotel.................................921 (C1)
Welcome Inn..................................359 (H4)
Woodley Hotel 113 (E4)

BUSINESS DIRECTORY

MACHINING & MACHINERY

Boston Metal & Machinery Co	196 (K5)
Denny's Welding Shop	484 (E3)
Pauline Millinery Imptr	812 (B3)
Rau Fastener Co	918 (H4)

MEDICAL

Chaffin Lawrence Dr	135 (M2)
Chaffin Rafe C MD	412 (F1)
Denton's Pharmacy	164 (I5)
Dresser Walter P Dr	821 (A2)
Glen Haven Sanitarium	382 (N5)
Janar Pharmacy	623 (D2)
Raulston Burrell O Dr	976 (I2)
St John Valentine Dr	132 (L6)
St Louis Drug Co	576 (B3)
St Vincent's Hospital	531 (C6)
Swan A H MD	515 (F6)
Welch Sylvester H MD	173 (J3)
Welfer C R Dr	309 (L2)
Woodlawn Pharmacy	235 (A6)
Victoria Square Drug	255 (N3)

NEWSPAPER

Los Angeles Examiner	014 (R3)
Los Angeles Standard	016 (L2)
Los Angeles Times	169 (L4)

POST OFFICES

Adams & Arlington	339 (H6)
Beverly & Santa Monica	433 (B3)
Cochran & Jefferson	438 (E6)
Gardner & Third	003 (D1)
Fairfax & Sunset	335 (E1)
Normandie & Hollywood	008 (I2)
Olive & 4th	924 (N3)
Pico & Hauser	402 (J5)
Pico & Warner	929 (A5)
Sunset & Alemeda	902 (E4)
Wilshire & Grand	338 (O2)
Wilshire & June	313 (G3)

PRINTING & COPY SERVICES

Ayers Printing Co	182 (H3)
Back Number Newspaper Co	104 (I6)
Drenk Poster-Print Co	235 (G4)
James United Photo Serv	174 (F2)

RESTAURANTS

Athletic Club	099 (F4)
Big Boy Burgers	122 (D2)
Blue Wave	074 (C6)
Boston Tavern	592 (M6)
Delmonico's	188 (H1)
Frank's Pizza House	065 (B3)
Glassman's Delicatessen	585 (D6)
Lucky Domenic's	219 (A5)
Moon Chop Suey Parlor	882 (G3)
Pauline's Pantry	930 (Q1)
Russo Super Club	016 (G1)
Sidewalk Cafe	404 (H1)
The Brown Derby	049 (K8)
The Falcon	789 (F4)
The Pilot	848 (A3)
The Spinning Wheel	711 (B5)
The Tuck Shop	418 (C6)
Trocadero Nightclub	045 (D1)
Welcome Chop Suey Cafe	852 (D4)

SERVICES

Awning Studios	292 (M4)
Babylon Oriental Rug Cleaners	281 (P4)
Bachmann P J Picture Framing	375 (D3)
Bosch Radio Repair & Sales Co	586 (D5)
Bossin Upholstering Co	810 (G6)
Dreiss Alarm Co	274 (L5)
Drewes William F Amer Florist	554 (C1)
Montroy Electrical Mfg Co	498 (M5)
Paulis-Staples Co	919 (O3)

SPORTS

Bilton Boxing Club	712 (N2)
Civic Arena	918 (B5)
Hollywood Bowls!	285 (G2)
Wrigley Field	212 (A5)

TOBACCONIST

News & Cigar	089 (N8)

TRANSPORTATION SERVICES

LA Cab Co	015 (L4)
Pan American Travel Agency	571 (O1)

RESIDENTIAL DIRECTORY

A

Name	Address
Aalto, E, J	812 (D2)
Abbott, E, W	655 (L4)
Abbott, Harris	354 (N3)
Abernathy, B, S	298 (Q4)
Abraham, R, H	840 (D1)
Ackerman, Jno, D	084 (C5)
Adams, Mrs, G, T	382 (J3)
Adams, E, S	574 (J3)
Adams, Prof, J, J	807 (J5)
Adamson, Mrs, M	166 (G1)
Agen, O, D	861 (D6)
Ah, Bon	133 (A1)
Ah, Ping	327 (D3)
Ah, Kim, Gue	989 (R1)
Ahlin, H, A	481 (D1)
Ahrens, Mitz	644 (R1)
Aikin, Dr, I, B	968 (O5)
Aitken, J, C	542 (O6)
Albanis, George	353 (G5)
Albin, I	827 (Q4)
Albrecht, H, M	266 (L2)
Albright, J, W	763 (G6)
Alden, Jr, B, W	589 (M5)
Alder, Albt	613 (N1)
Alderman, A	787 (P4)
Allen, Douglas	661 (I2)
Allen, Andy	417 (I3)
Allen, Mrs, Marie	395 (N4)
Allen, Mrs, H	309 (R3)
Andereggen, Mrs	745 (B2)
Anderson, Fred	174 (F2)
Anderson, E, C	235 (G4)
Anderson, A, T	182 (H3)
Anderson, D, F	104 (I6)
Anderson, Pauline	488 (N2)
Anderson, Mrs, S	642 (Q2)
Andrews, Nick	933 (H4)
Andrews, P	905 (B2)
Andrews, Mrs, J	077 (R5)
Angel, S	549 (Q4)
Annand, E	821 (L4)
Annaz, S	200 (O1)
Anthony, M, P	993 (Q2)
Antone, S, J	452 (F2)
Aprahanian, A	708 (G6)
Arena, Prank	416 (H3)
Arena, S	428 (I6)
Arey, Mrs, Lucy	882 (K4)
Armour, Mrs, J	415 (H4)
Armstrong, J, M	889 (A5)
Armstrong, Mrs, E	289 (G2)
Arthur, Otto	342 (K4)
Ashby, Stanley	539 (J1)
Ashford, Mrs, L	484 (O4)
Avon, Santo	068 (H3)
Avon, John	156 (Q3)
Avonde, Henry	106 (K3)
Awoki, Tom	289 (M5)
Awrey, Bruce, B	246 (L5)
Axe, Harry, D	065 (E2)
Axe, Jr, Paul, W	542 (K5)
Axe, Fred	487 (L6)
Axelford, C, L	433 (F5)
Axelrod, S, I	844 (D3)
Axelrod, Diane	644 (D5)
Axelrod, Joe	183 (M5)
Axelrode, Sam	223 (Q2)
Axelson, John	328 (B4)
Axler, Harry	713 (D4)
Axley, Feliz, J	518 (H4)
Axline, Joseph, T	578 (Q2)
Axtell, Ethel, M	484 (D1)
Axtell, Edgar, H	087 (H1)
Axtell, Miss, B	063 (H1)
Aydelotte, Veda	836 (O2)
Aye, Robt, D	397 (O2)
Aye, Elias, J	297 (P2)
Ayer, Philip, E	517 (D3)
Ayer, Peggy	868 (I5)
Ayer, Ann	406 (O5)
Ayer, Cecelia	935 (P4)
Ayer, Miss, Ann	788 (Q4)
Ayeroff, Aaron	827 (E5)
Ayers, Harry, O	933 (D1)
Ayers, Mrs, Alice	460 (E3)
Ayers, Mrs, C, G	890 (I3)
Ayers, Marian	781 (J2)
Ayers, Florence, E	355 (J3)
Ayers, Ben	197 (M5)
Ayers, Frank, W	921 (Q3)
Aykroyd, Jr, J, W	119 (C6)
Aylesworth, Arthur	781 (C3)
Aylett, Darrell, H	104 (H4)
Ayling, Thomas, A	819 (R5)
Aylmer, Leroy, A	480 (H5)
Aylward, Milo, D	203 (J3)
Aylward, Miss, H	532 (K5)
Aylward, Julian, T	100 (L3)

B

Name	Address
Babick, Matthew	792 (H2)
Babin, Erwin	277 (D2)
Babington, David	847 (M5)
Babior, Louis, A	825 (F3)
Babior, Sonia	068 (G1)
Babitz, Jr, Nathan	436 (O5)
Babo, John	421 (D4)
Babsky, Mrs, Rose	131 (H3)
Babson, Horace, P	855 (D4)
Baca, Frank, S	414 (C4)
Baca, Leon, S	636 (G5)
Baca, Alfred	254 (P3)
Bacarella, Jim	913 (N6)
Bachmann, A, M	259 (C2)
Bachmann, Philip, J	139 (K2)
Bachmeyer, Carl, J	939 (D3)
Bachrach, M	167 (H4)
Bachrach, Mrs, R	771 (L3)
Bachrack, H, A	846 (A2)
Bachtel, Earl	629 (C5)
Bachtel, Clara	809 (P5)
Bachtell, Robt	313 (A1)
Bachtell, Sidney, N	582 (B6)
Bacigalupi, Jr, L	842 (G1)
Bacigalupi, Berto	868 (P1)
Bacile, Jack	764 (I5)
Back, Clara	045 (D1)
Back, Hattie	730 (Q1)
Backall, Lewis	693 (H5)
Backensto, F, E	513 (C2)
Backer, Paul	885 (B3)
Backer, Wanda, A	534 (H1)
Backhoff, Henry	923 (C1)
Backlund, Gordon	076 (O3)
Backman, Arletta	919 (I2)
Baker, M, S	267 (F3)
Baldwin, E, S	814 (N4)
Ball, Chester, H	683 (H3)
Ball, H, H	457 (P5)
Ballard, B, W	523 (G2)
Balls, John, G	465 (G1)
Bancroft, Mrs, H	918 (G5)
Banfield, J, T	650 (F6)
Bankhead, D, B	267 (J3)
Bankhead, Mrs	785 (M6)
Banks, O, C	694 (H4)
Barber, Edgar, H	933 (G2)
Barnett, Phillip	919 (F1)
Bednarz, Albt	779 (G4)
Beebe, Eva, L	199 (N4)
Been, Sangr	745 (R2)
Begley, Mrs, F	532 (A5)
Bekins, Abe	201 (Q4)
Belden, Jud, S	371 (C5)

RESIDENTIAL DIRECTORY

Belden, W 605 (K5)
Bell, Dr, Harold.........882 (E5)
Bell, C, A....................221 (L4)
Bell, J, H....................204 (N4)
Belli, Enis 500 (I1)
Belling, L....................595 (D2)
Bellmer, H, T.............095 (L3)
Belmont, Mrs, L, J 448 (E2)
Belrose, W, X 085 (A5)
Belvel, Jones 448 (R3)
Bickford, O, L.............858 (J3)
Big, Charley 257 (H3)
Bigelow, L, E 423 (F5)
Bilger, F, W...............830 (L4)
Billings, Mary, W 755 (O6)
Binder, Louis 342 (C6)
Bing, Kong, Tong 405 (M4)
Bingham, W, H..........062 (M3)
Blagelow, Mrs, F, C 370 (D4)
Blanchard, C..............997 (Q1)
Blank, Mrs, Kay..........297 (B2)
Blanton, Mrs, C..........473 (J6)
Blazier, Mrs, A 338 (D5)
Blumstein, S 664 (A3)
Bock, M.....................642 (E4)
Bode, Julius 610 (H4)
Boehn, M, E...............377 (C5)
Boehrer, Mrs, M.........237 (N6)
Boener, Frank............808 (Q2)
Bohannon, Dr, J, L 426 (D5)
Bohnet, P...................872 (F3)
Boies, Geo, V 913 (Q4)
Bolton, T, L...............862 (O3)
Bonino, Dr, F 879 (D5)
Bonn, Ralph, E...........723 (I2)
Bootsma, Wm, A 384 (C3)
Borchard, Fred...........236 (F4)
Borgstron, Mrs, John 764 (M1)
Borne, Mrs, Laura......323 (E6)
Borrel, Chaz 228 (E4)
Bosbyshell, Miss, C....260 (H4)
Bosch, Cyril, E 702 (J3)
Boschan, Louis, E 075 (C3)
Boschan, Mrs, F........108 (R2)
Bosche, Mrs, A 803 (G5)
Boscus, J, M 962 (C4)
Bose, Ada, V 788 (G5)
Bose, Miss, T.............525 (K6)
Boselly, E, M.............696 (N2)
Boshardt, Harry.........049 (N3)
Boshes, Philip............635 (E4)
Bosio, Cristforo 986 (E5)

Bosio, Asunta............892 (H2)
Boskey, Miss, H.........382 (Q5)
Bosko, Bob 734 (J2)
Bosler, Joseph, G 176 (E3)
Bosler, Harlan 482 (G2)
Bosler, Ethel 370 (M1)
Bosley, Mabel............682 (B5)
Bosley, Leola 625 (G1)
Boslough, M, C..........148 (N4)
Bosman, Ford 302 (I6)
Bossert, Fred.............670 (F5)
Bosshard, Mrs, J 244 (B5)
Bosshard, A, H..........266 (H1)
Bosshard, Mrs, M 352 (P5)
Bosson, C, C 221 (F5)
Bossuet, Philana 459 (G6)
Bossuot, Lena 420 (D6)
Bost, Linda, M 336 (B3)
Bostick, Miss, V 938 (N5)
Bostler, Miss, B 171 (C2)
Boston, Mrs, A...........340 (M5)
Boston, Grace, E 478 (R2)
Bosworth, B, P 770 (R4)
Bothwell, R, C 405 (F4)
Botsford, G, A 977 (C5)
Boulin, F, A 284 (I1)
Bovyer, W, B 134 (A5)
Bow, Hing, Wo 474 (L1)
Bowen, Mrs, E, M 841 (C2)
Bowers, J, L 458 (Q3)
Bowersmith, O 869 (N1)
Bowne, M..................717 (C6)
Boyd, T, J 320 (H1)
Boyle, D, M 273 (F2)
Bradshaw, Mrs, F 943 (B5)
Brady, Mrs, M 423 (D4)
Braendlin, J, C 641 (D3)
Braiuard, Geo, L 913 (F6)
Brandes, A, R F.........129 (A3)
Branthaver, H, B........247 (H3)
Brause, F, W 468 (N1)
Brawley, J, E 296 (N1)
Bridges, H, M............794 (G4)
Brier, X, W 295 (Q4)
Bright, Wm 282 (A5)
Bright, C, A 261 (N2)
Brink, Dr, H, O 046 (Q2)
Brnnner, B, B 546 (G3)
Broadway..................498 (Q6)
Brock, Eugene, L........464 (G2)
Broderick, Mrs, J 355 (C6)
Brodt, Miss, A 338 (F3)

Brooks, W, R.............603 (D3)
Brophy, S...................292 (N2)
Brown, P, A 250 (C1)
Brown, A...................555 (G6)
Brown, Mrs, E, M 931 (K1)
Burlage, Carl 017 (N4)

C

Cessna, Sam.............227 (K5)
Ceurvorst, John.........765 (H6)
Cevola, A 738 (K6)
Cezar, Mrs, M............392 (J6)
Cezon, Pedro.............579 (A5)
Chabot, Frank...........229 (E3)
Chabot, Emma..........784 (R2)
Chabre, A, A 311 (M5)
Chabre, Louis, P........777 (Q4)
Chace, Harry, B.........674 (A3)
Chace, Chas, H..........794 (D5)
Chacel, Miss, A.........246 (C3)
Chadbourn, Mrs, E....354 (C3)
Chadbourne, R, F.......476 (F1)
Chadburn, Mrs, F......969 (H1)
Chaddock, Frank.......233 (H3)
Chaddock, H, F..........281 (I2)
Chadduck, K..............437 (L5)
Chaderton, O M........257 (H6)
Chadez, Johm 452 (E6)
Chadil, Edwin, A 836 (R5)
Chadima, John..........437 (R3)
Chadney, Will 166 (A5)
Chadnow, Chas, K 248 (A1)
Chadsey, Miss, F 752 (R4)
Chadwick, Mrs, E.......284 (F2)
Chadwick, E, L..........530 (H4)
Chadwick, G, R..........601 (O5)
Chadwick, Mrs, E.......663 (Q5)
Chaffey, Ben 142 (B2)
Chaffey, Ned 317 (F6)
Chaffin, Glenn 044 (G3)
Chaffin, L..................174 (P5)
Chagi, Saml..............102 (P3)
Chaiken, Isabelle.......197 (K4)
Chaikin, Mrs, S..........788 (Q2)
Chaillaux, B, S 607 (C2)
Chaillaux, Homer......169 (L4)
Chaille, Mrs, L 475 (D6)
Chaimovitz, H 478 (D2)
Chain, A, P 743 (I6)
Chais, George, J 214 (D1)
Chait, Harry 115 (G3)
Chaix, Ed..................658 (E6)

RESIDENTIAL DIRECTORY

Chaix, Frank.............671 (L3)
Chakov, Rose.............779 (J2)
Chaler, Marie.............489 (N5)
Chalfant, Paul, M.....822 (G6)
Chalfant, Mrs, A.....840 (L2)
Chalfin, Mrs, S, A.....309 (D2)
Chalfin, Harry.............274 (R3)
Chalif, Selmer, L.....516 (D5)
Chalk, Ruth.............794 (E5)
Chalk, James, N.....402 (M1)
Chalker, Jack.............139 (D4)
Chalker, Sidney, T.....816 (Q4)
Chee, Dong.............705 (E1)
Chin, Pook.............084 (E3)
Chin, Dim.............110 (L3)
Chin, Chong.............817 (Q3)
Chong, Yuen.............406 (M1)
Clinton, Clifford.......101 (O4)
Cobb, J.............368 (A6)
Coburn, J, A.............990 (L5)
Cochran, H, L.............282 (N1)
Coelho, A.............888 (P6)
Cohn, Mrs, E.............793 (K5)
Coin, Mrs, F.............519 (E3)
Coit, R.............158 (I5)
Colby, Mrs, S, E.....725 (F1)
Cole, Mrs, C, D.....944 (L3)
Coley, V, J.............826 (K4)
Collin, B, M.............812 (F5)
Collins, Clyde.............466 (B2)
Collins, John.............739 (I3)
Colson, C.............321 (R3)
Conant, Harris.............637 (N3)
Condon, C, E.............442 (C5)
Congdon, M, S.............758 (Q3)
Conger, H, E.............423 (I4)
Conn, E.............302 (H5)
Conner, L, W.............612 (A4)
Connett, A, P.............660 (Q1)
Connie, Mrs.............516 (F2)
Connolly, Mrs, P, J.....601 (K6)
Conway, Mrs, H, M...133 (G4)
Cook, J.............586 (A3)
Cook, C, A.............698 (D1)
Cook, Norman, D.....611 (K2)
Cook, Mrs, Chas.......678 (L2)
Coombs, A, G.............527 (O1)
Cooper, Geo, D.........780 (E5)
Cooper, Sarah.............568 (I5)
Cope, Mrs, J.............752 (C5)
Copeland, Mrs, A.....202 (P6)
Copmaun, Mrs.............096 (J2)

Corbett, Mrs, J...........115 (M5)
Corder, Mrs, F, J.....516 (R5)
Corgiat, John.............855 (I6)
Cornell, D, J.............452 (D2)
Corpe, W, R.............527 (B5)
Cortez, J.............908 (C7)
Corwin, G, W.............351 (H5)
Courant, Mrs, F.............328 (C5)
Covert, Leonard.......061 (B1)
Cowan, C, W.............830 (E1)
Cox, Mrs, F, M.............184 (D1)
Coz, Mrs, M.............903 (K6)
Cozad, S, W.............802 (C6)
Craib, Mrs, E.............916 (P3)
Craig, David.............973 (C2)
Craker, R, J.............734 (P5)
Cram, C, C.............528 (R3)
Crane, Ida.............010 (M4)
Crawford, E, A.............880 (E3)
Crean, C, F.............648 (H5)
Cretser, Miss, M.....681 (A2)
Cretser, Gale, O.....288 (F1)
Crocker, Mrs, M.....434 (Q1)
Cron, Miss, M.............213 (E1)
Crook, Si, Anne.........806 (D5)
Cross, C, W.............271 (K3)
Crossley, Nat, M.....265 (L2)
Crouch, Miss, M.....372 (G5)
Crowell, Clarence....789 (I6)
Cruest, Wm.............237 (A3)
Cruze, Robt.............234 (H4)
Culbertson, B, O.....447 (P6)
Cullen, Mrs, R, B.......093 (R4)
Culligan, Will, J.....221 (H4)
Cunha, L, J.............067 (C1)
Cunning, Howard.....191 (C3)
Cunningham, Wm...750 (H3)
Cunningham, E.............289 (N4)
Curran, B, N.............095 (H3)
Currier, Frank, G.....115 (C3)
Curtis, L, F.............977 (M2)

D

Dai, Dong.............239 (K5)
Dalains, G.............683 (O4)
Dalto, Frank.............466 (P6)
Daly, John, E.............809 (K5)
Daly, Tina.............574 (M6)
Damianakes, C.............346 (P4)
Daniel, R.............465 (H2)
Daniels, J, W.............851 (A1)
Danielson, C, B.............578 (G2)

Dashwood, Mrs, T.....218 (P1)
Daul, Mrs, W.............437 (G6)
Davenport, P, D.....394 (M4)
Davidson, F.............391 (N4)
Davis, Mrs, C, C.....146 (A4)
Davis, Gordon.............403 (F6)
Davis, J, C.............782 (G5)
Davis, Frank, A.............701 (J2)
Davis, Mrs, Jessie.....419 (J2)
Davis, Wm, F.............305 (O2)
Dawson, S, B.............351 (A5)
De Albergaria, S.....843 (C1)
De Caccia, W, C.....809 (G4)
De Costa, Frank.............966 (K2)
De Faria, Dr, J, B.....253 (C2)
De La Rue, Dr, E.....109 (E2)
De Mers, Leo, A.....208 (K4)
De Norght, Allie.....769 (Q3)
De Normandie, S.....863 (F5)
De Noville, Z, V.....577 (G2)
De Nubila, Mrs, T.....792 (R6)
De Nufrio, Dan.............336 (Q5)
De Nully, Mrs, R.....106 (D2)
De Nunzio, Elvira.....491 (F5)
De Nunzio, T, M.....780 (G4)
De Nure, Walter, B.....949 (N3)
De Olazabal, M.....382 (C5)
De Paemelaere, S.....943 (Q1)
De Palkowska, M.....701 (D1)
De Palma, Rose.............255 (A6)
De Palma, John.............642 (K4)
De Palma, Clara.............452 (O4)
De Pass, S, C.............575 (Q4)
De Roco, Mrs, J.....629 (D1)
Deakin, G.............656 (C4)
Dean, Chas, A.............082 (D4)
Dearborn, F, K.............137 (F6)
Deasy, Thomas.............834 (D2)
Dechow, C, C.............896 (L5)
Dee, Hing.............089 (B7)
Dee, Bing.............554 (H3)
Dee, Sam.............767 (P1)
Deeney, Geo, F.............979 (H3)
Del Martin, N, A.....055 (C4)
Delaney, Mrs, W, F.....495 (L4)
Delmas, F.............741 (M3)
DeMartini, Mrs, P.....607 (C4)
Demos, Geo.............960 (O3)
Denison, Geo, H.....302 (R3)
Denney, R, G.............497 (P4)
Dennison, Mrs, S.....852 (D4)
Dennison, Mrs, F.....333 (F4)

RESIDENTIAL DIRECTORY

Dennison, Ray, O 350 (I2)
Dennison, H 097 (L5)
Dennison, Mrs, R 849 (P2)
Denniston, Rose, M .. 924 (N3)
Denny, Elna 432 (B5)
Denny, Jack 128 (C5)
Denny, Myrtle, V 227 (I4)
Denny, Roy 704 (L5)
Denny, Virginia 284 (Q6)
Denoyer, Mrs, Julia ... 196 (G6)
Densham, Thos 303 (Q6)
Denslow, Fred 263 (H1)
Denslow, Clyde, B ... 611 (Q3)
Densmore, Eileen 992 (E2)
Densmore, M, H 449 (K2)
Densmore, Claire 437 (Q1)
Denson, Pete 248 (C5)
Denson, Grace, R 681 (G4)
Denton, William, J ... 403 (O5)
Denyer, Albt, G 118 (E3)
Denzer, Chas, D 802 (B5)
Denzer, David, G 181 (F6)
Denzer, J, A 203 (O3)
Denzin, Chas, W 795 (I2)
Denzin, Mrs, M, H ... 238 (O3)
Deocampo, S, G 135 (M2)
Deom, Georgette 412 (F1)
Deong, Pong 821 (A2)
Depoli, J 249 (E5)
Derrick, Dr, Geo, H ... 736 (D5)
Detels, Hing, D 273 (J6)
Deung, Hee, J 460 (C2)
Deveny, H 402 (E3)
Dew, Hing 328 (N1)
Deward, Geo, C 474 (C3)
Dewson, Mrs, V, A ... 332 (C5)
Dhnond, M 361 (Q3)
Di, Dung 256 (F2)
Dickins, Charles, P ... 567 (J3)
Dickinson, John 559 (A3)
Dieve, Mrs, B, J A ... 596 (E4)
Digger, Miss, Mary ... 233 (P4)
Dill, C, B 953 (J4)
Dimaline, H, A 818 (L4)
Dinneen, B 627 (B6)
Dixon, Wesley 263 (G2)
Dodge, Mrs, ... 660 (M2)
Doell, Carl 441 (R4)
Dolan, Geo, J 356 (H5)
Dollings, A, A 493 (F1)
Donaldson, W 146 (E1)
Donaughey, J, H 484 (L5)

Dong, Hen 111 (P6)
Donnelly, Dr, Geo 226 (H5)
Donogh, T, J 069 (D3)
Donogh, A, O 748 (F4)
Dooley, Ethel 601 (P3)
Doone , Alice 888 (C6)
Dorsch, Mrs, Chas ... 053 (B3)
Dougherty, A 402 (B1)
Douglas, Mrs, M 338 (N2)
Dowdle, Clara, L 323 (D3)
Downey, Mrs, F 880 (C5)
Downing, T, J 736 (P4)
Doyle, Faye 639 (L2)
Dragicivich, John ... 761 (I6)
Drake, Cecil 226 (N1)
Drakos, Peter 377 (A3)
Dreaper, Calvin, P ... 341 (G5)
Dreier, Gus, J 777 (K1)
Dreifus, August 931 (F3)
Dreiling, Chas 720 (F1)
Dreisbach, G, W 577 (D2)
Dreiske, Louis, F 775 (Q5)
Dreiss, John, H 520 (A6)
Drell, John, R 182 (F2)
Drell, Louis 332 (G3)
Drengberg, J, H 171 (C2)
Drennan, Jayne 094 (C4)
Drennan, Mrs, S 692 (Q1)
Drennen, Seiph, E ... 932 (G3)
Drennen, H, F 542 (P6)
Drenth, John 889 (J4)
Dresbach, Roy 507 (G3)
Dresback, M, J 379 (I6)
Drescher, Rob 683 (A3)
Drescher, Martha ... 127 (I3)
Dresman, Frank, J ... 389 (J6)
Dresner, Mrs, I 699 (H3)
Dresow, Mrs, Celia ... 434 (A6)
Dresser, Walter, E ... 049 (B2)
Dresser, John, G 183 (E3)
Dresser, Edward, L ... 412 (H3)
Dresser, Harry, B ... 966 (I4)
Drew, Thomas 560 (E4)
Drew, John, F 957 (G5)
Drew, Mrs, G 598 (N4)
Drew, Mrs, M 559 (N5)
Drewes, Katherine ... 849 (F5)
Drewes, W, J 227 (M2)
Drewett, Saml, J ... 298 (O4)
Drews, Harley, F ... 567 (D4)
Drews, Herb 711 (M3)
Drews, Mrs, Hazel ... 519 (N2)

Drexel, Gertrude 413 (B3)
Drey, Mike 773 (F5)
Drey, Bert 405 (L5)
Dreyer, Geo, J 508 (O3)
Dreyer, Mrs, John ... 725 (I5)
Dreyer, Henry, H ... 809 (L5)
Dreyer, Dave 841 (M3)
Dreyer, George, U ... 598 (Q3)
Dreyfus, Ned 801 (E1)
Dreyfus, Frieda 312 (I2)
Dreyzehnew, E 158 (H4)
Drha, Mrs, Marie ... 687 (J1)
Driemeyer, John, H ... 740 (H2)
Driver, Mrs, George ... 500 (R2)
Druhan, Mrs, T, P ... 733 (L3)
Du, Mrs, Quesne ... 523 (G3)
Dubovsky, M 331 (G6)
Duesler, G, H 480 (D4)
Dugan, Mrs, T, H ... 364 (K5)
Duncan, C, F 514 (G4)
Duncan, J, C 589 (R4)
Dunham, Mrs, I 566 (M6)
Dunn, J, C 943 (I2)
Dunster, Mrs, G 585 (Q5)
Dupont, Blanche ... 743 (J2)
Dupree, Mrs, Leo ... 312 (A4)
Durant, Mrs, D, W ... 195 (A4)
Durggan, G, E 787 (Q5)
Dutchler, Geo, A ... 890 (F1)

E

Ebbesen, C 316 (H4)
Eckley, P, M 225 (R6)
Ede, R, H 130 (Q5)
Edgar, J, J 661 (A5)
Edger, R 650 (C1)
Edmondson, C, T ... 844 (M6)
Edson, J, H 889 (A4)
Edwards, J, W 298 (M3)
Edwards, W, H 290 (P3)
Egenberger, V 905 (D6)
Eglesich, Nick 600 (M2)
Ehlert, Chas, H 297 (K1)
Ehret, Eugene 102 (K3)
Eiben, F, G 356 (R4)
Elam, Mrs, Edie, L ... 016 (G1)
Elardy, Harry 130 (A5)
Elder, R 151 (F3)
Eliason, H, A 768 (F6)
Ellena, Jos 974 (E1)
Elliot, Albt, H 729 (L4)
Elliott, John, S 948 (H4)

RESIDENTIAL DIRECTORY

Ellis, Mrs, Fred, H 213 (A6)
Ellis, Bros.....................819 (P5)
Elmer, Mrs, M, O........229 (E4)
Elrod, J, R....................747 (A2)
Elston, C, N..................269 (O5)
Embury, J, V 654 (J1)
Emery, Mrs, C, F 100 (N6)
Emeryville, Stable........890 (L1)
Eoberson, Mrs, E 358 (P4)
Eoullet, G 528 (O3)
Epperson, H, T.............260 (P6)
Epstein, Joe..................369 (N2)
Erickson, G...................439 (K5)
Ericsson, Prof, Carl.....325 (D6)
Erskine, Howard 472 (I2)
Eschbacher, W, P.........779 (R5)
Esposito, P...................155 (O2)
Esterbrook, G, G 317 (L1)
Estrada, P, B................666 (P5)
Etnier, Mrs, Bessie 623 (E3)
Evans, Harry 561 (B5)
Evans, Ernest 962 (D1)
Evans, C.......................617 (G2)

F

Fagalde, J, E 832 (H5)
Fairbanks, A, A............889 (E2)
Fairchild, A, E 724 (R2)
Fairly, R, B..................646 (Q2)
Fazande, Mrs, W 283 (G6)
Feathers, Mrs, C..........566 (R6)
Feierbach, Mrs, A 453 (N4)
Felkel, Alois, J.............493 (F5)
Fendrich, J...................166 (C2)
Fenton, J, M 287 (O3)
Fenwick, W, B 369 (N5)
Ferguson, Alice 276 (N6)
Ferguson, H..................691 (Q4)
Fernandez, John...........321 (M1)
Ferrier, Francis 932 (G5)
Ferris, Mrs, Geo 996 (O6)
Feswick, F 013 (M4)
Fetherolf, A 365 (Q2)
Fhilbrick, H, M 577 (F5)
Field, Mrs, H, N............796 (D3)
Field, Mrs, K 572 (I1)
Fields , Miss, M 809 (F6)
Figone, Frank...............222 (C6)
Figone, L......................921 (L4)
Filley, Mrs, A, J 942 (N6)
Fillmore, Mary, F 700 (E5)
Finidori, D, S 711 (G1)

Finkelstein, J 070 (C2)
Finney, E, James 539 (C4)
Firpo, J.........................149 (H1)
Flaherty, T, J................487 (L4)
Flannigan, Mrs, M.......782 (Q4)
Fleck, A, G 344 (N6)
Flemming, Mrs, A........255 (H4)
Fletcher, W, C..............416 (M5)
Fletcher , Joe 509 (F4)
Flinker, Mrs, J 422 (O4)
Flinn, J, W 846 (I4)
Florence, Mrs, E...........250 (C6)
Fluth, J, H 067 (D3)
Flynn, Mrs, Jos 896 (C6)
Focht, Mrs, E 234 (A1)
Foley, J, J 192 (A3)
Foley, O, L 090 (H2)
Fonda, Mrs, J, C..........507 (B5)
Fontaine, A, A 662 (B5)
Foo, Woo 097 (D2)
Foo, Qui, Chin 617 (I3)
Forbes, Henry 738 (B2)
Ford, C, W B................427 (J2)
Fordim , Walter 774 (A5)
Forneris, C 889 (N5)
Forrest, F, C 531 (F6)
Forry, Geo, A 770 (O3)
Forsyth, J, W 089 (M2)
Foss, F, W 748 (P4)
Foster, Chas.................431 (H2)
Foster, L.......................198 (I5)
Foubert, Mrs, E, J 800 (Q2)
Fowler, Warren, C 829 (D5)
Fowler, Miss, A, B 612 (N2)
Fox, Geo, F 143 (D1)
Fox, Mrs, J 875 (H5)
Frates , Li, J.................837 (I5)
Frazer, H, L 130 (K2)
Frederick, Dr, F, A........557 (F3)
Freeburn, Dyson 253 (L4)
Freitas, A 298 (L1)
Freitas, J, C 383 (R3)
Frescott, Mrs, K 673 (L4)
Fricke, Dr, Richd..........796 (N6)
Friedman, A.................410 (H2)
Friedrich, Otto 444 (E1)
Frimmer, Mrs, E 245 (J4)
Friz, Eugene 811 (A2)
Fry, J, W 417 (H3)
Fugel, Peter 788 (H1)
Fuji, Boy 182 (A5)

G

Gable, Clark.................037 (B2)
Gallagher, Mrs, W ...521 (C4)
Gallagher, T, F 437 (E5)
Gallet, Mrs, B, M 946 (R4)
Gallot, Mrs, L 540 (H4)
Gamble, W, J 621 (B5)
Gandara, Juan.............611 (F3)
Garcia, F.......................133 (F6)
Garden, Carl................479 (F1)
Gardiner, W, E 973 (B2)
Gargurevich, Luke.....780 (E2)
Garretson, H, W 788 (P2)
Gassoomis, Gus...........239 (P4)
Gates, A, Livery............862 (G5)
Gaul, O, J 728 (G2)
Gaylord, H, S...............480 (O5)
Gazanego, John 978 (F4)
Gearing, Mrs, M 949 (D4)
Geddes, Mrs, A...........650 (M5)
Gee, Sack 719 (A4)
Gee, Shing...................159 (R2)
Gee-Hing, John 392 (L3)
Geer, Mrs, Chas 828 (B4)
Gehrke, C.....................746 (D3)
Gelder, L......................814 (N4)
Gemmiti, R, Q 374 (F5)
Genick, John................055 (G4)
George, Dowe..............543 (N6)
Gerard, B, H 862 (A4)
Gerhardt, Mrs 056 (M4)
Gernreich, E 931 (Q4)
Gerow, A, F 400 (K6)
Getchell, W, J 388 (D6)
Geussi, B......................637 (N4)
Ghigliotti, A 947 (G2)
Ghirardelli, Mrs............292 (R2)
Giacopetti, Mrs............357 (N6)
Giamtoruno, Mrs..........194 (F4)
Gibhs, Mrs, B 883 (A4)
Gibson, C, D 646 (F1)
Gibson, H, E 839 (J5)
Gier, Theo....................549 (E5)
Gilbert, Miss, G............646 (B5)
Gilbert, Mrs, Lutie ...870 (J2)
Gillam, J......................694 (H3)
Gillette, J, E 818 (G3)
Gilstrap, Mrs, L, I 092 (P1)
Gim, Wing, Chong....560 (E3)
Gin, How, Toy 334 (D5)
Ginochio, J, B...............085 (C4)

RESIDENTIAL DIRECTORY

Gioia, Louis 168 (C1)
Girdwood, B, B 147 (K3)
Giuffre, J 663 (M6)
Gladfelter, C, S 793 (I5)
Glass, Miss, Buby 163 (R3)
Glassman, Sam 788 (F2)
Glassman, Saml 976 (I2)
Glasso, Leola 132 (L6)
Glasson, Thomas 515 (F6)
Glaszman, G 173 (J3)
Glatstein, S 309 (L2)
Glatt, Joe 531 (C6)
Glatt, Mrs, M 164 (I5)
Glatt, William 382 (N5)
Glatte, Hayden 623 (D2)
Glattenberg, Mrs 576 (B3)
Glatzau, Albt, M 235 (A6)
Glauber, Myron, J 730 (F1)
Glaum, Phyllis 989 (J3)
Glauninger, M, M 274 (M4)
Glavas, Andrew, A 153 (N5)
Glave, Mary, C 488 (F2)
Glavecke, Miss, F 799 (R3)
Glaviano, D 131 (E5)
Glaviano, Nick 447 (K4)
Glavin, William, F 964 (C2)
Glavinic, Mrs, L 292 (M4)
Glaw, W, J 281 (P4)
Glazbrook, C, S 375 (D3)
Glaze, Austin, O 586 (D5)
Glaze, Robt 132 (G6)
Glazer, Miss, Jean 274 (L5)
Glazier, Harry, M 554 (C1)
Glazier, Corydon, J 498 (M5)
Gleason, Mrs, Vera 484 (E3)
Gleason, Mrs, M 196 (K5)
Gleason, M 919 (O3)
Gleaves, Laura, C 839 (C6)
Gleckner, Harry, J 170 (O5)
Gledhill, Jeff 203 (F2)
Gledhill, Mrs, H, J 128 (M4)
Gleed, Mrs, James 717 (M5)
Gleeksman, Louis 280 (J5)
Gleerup, Otto 812 (N3)
Gleeson, T 469 (J4)
Gleichen, Carl 461 (M1)
Gleiforst, Fred, A 102 (B1)
Gleim, Perry, M 916 (K1)
Gleim, John, H 962 (N3)
Gleis, Michael 456 (G5)
Gleis, Ben 817 (P5)
Glen, Oaks 472 (F2)

Glen, Mrs, J, A 241 (R6)
Glenar, Sid 412 (D6)
Glibert, Geo, J 857 (P2)
Goldwater, Mrs, Y 930 (F3)
Gomez, Antone 812 (B3)
Gonzales, L, B 918 (H4)
Goodall, Mrs, B 970 (M2)
Goodman, Mrs, B 619 (F4)
Goodwin, H, L 718 (H6)
Goon, Yue 800 (R2)
Gordon, G, S 449 (G3)
Gori, W 143 (G6)
Gorman, M 063 (M4)
Goss, F, E 779 (D2)
Gottlieb, Mrs, M 160 (F3)
Gould, Mrs, C, A 606 (P6)
Gove, E, V 148 (M5)
Grabowski, A, J 830 (I3)
Graves, Nolan, T 011 (J4)
Gray, S &, F B 836 (C6)
Gray, Mrs, D 298 (F5)
Gray, Mrs, J, C 381 (L5)
Gray, Wm, A 264 (Q5)
Gray, Robt 586 (R3)
Grayson, Owen 756 (N3)
Greaney, J, E 376 (D3)
Grebs, Mrs, H 566 (G4)
Green, Mrs, C, W 163 (F4)
Gung, Yick 604 (F3)

H

Habnrt, Mrs, J 749 (O5)
Hadlen, C, P 896 (L4)
Haesloop, Mrs, H 809 (E5)
Hafner, Mrs, Chas 773 (A3)
Hagen, Will, A 348 (G5)
Haight, Fred, B 159 (F3)
Haines, Dan, W 521 (C5)
Haines, J, H 071 (F6)
Hair, Will, J 603 (H2)
Hale, W 789 (C6)
Haley, Wm, M 175 (M6)
Hall, Andrew 801 (J1)
Hall, C, E 960 (J3)
Hall, Robert 864 (Q4)
Hallahan, Mrs, M 021 (W4)
Hallett, Al, H 598 (H4)
Halpern, J 113 (E4)
Hamelin, W 359 (H4)
Hamilton, J, M 563 (F1)
Hansen, Cliarles 729 (C3)
Hansen, Miss, A 634 (M3)

Hanson, Mrs, G 797 (P2)
Hanson, Mrs, A 785 (P6)
Hanson, Silas 903 (R2)
Happ, W, J 235 (E2)
Haran, M, J 547 (E3)
Harano, M, G 075 (L3)
Harde, Grant, O 762 (A5)
Hartikainen, Peter 784 (L3)
Hartman, Mrs, W 188 (D3)
Hartung, A, J 474 (O1)
Hartz, John 937 (E6)
Harveston, Jos 311 (J1)
Haskell, W, P 339 (F2)
Hedenburg, G, F 594 (Q1)
Hedgpath, Mrs, S 152 (K4)
Hedley, Mrs, Van 465 (Q3)
Heeseman, C, J 186 (D4)
Heide, J 060 (I2)
Heinatz, Tom 363 (Q6)
Heinze, Mrs, Edw 093 (C4)
Heisterkamp, J 541 (N3)
Heleker , Emma 322 (H3)
Hellman, Ned 843 (K2)
Helmke, Chas, J 510 (Q5)
Helms, C, E 865 (Q3)
Hemenover, A 855 (G2)
Hen, Hong, Dow 387 (D4)
Henderson, Mrs 369 (G2)
Henderson, Mrs, E 268 (J2)
Henion, A, C 746 (Q2)
Henneberry, J, D 146 (I5)
Henninger, Mrs 634 (N2)
Henrich, Mrs, K 207 (E1)
Henrierues, M 696 (P3)
Henry, Mrs, A 421 (M3)
Herr, J G, Bell 795 (P5)
Herrick, C, W 654 (H4)
Herrlck, B, L 409 (L4)
Herskind, A 099 (N2)
Herzog, Mrs, C 459 (G5)
Hewes, G 176 (G1)
Hews, Geo, M 794 (P3)
Hi, Chong 648 (G5)
Hickman, A 035 (C3)
Hickox, Fred, S 777 (D3)
Hidecker, L 617 (F1)
Hie, Pung, A 817 (K2)
Hiett, W, I 337 (G4)
Higgins, Dr, I, W 592 (M6)
Hilgers, C, W 585 (D6)
Hill, J, A 882 (G3)
Hilling, E, H 930 (F4)

RESIDENTIAL DIRECTORY

Hilson, Dan, L 208 (Q1)
Hing, Kee 087 (I6)
Hinnian, J, M 676 (O4)
Hirschfeld, ... 353 (L4)
Hite, C, J 451 (H4)
Ho, Sing 284 (H5)
Hoey, Sam 034 (W4)
Hop, Wo, Dung 268 (B2)
How, Kee, W 373 (R3)
Hoy, On 332 (Q6)
Hub, J 290 (I2)
Hubbard, Miss, E 819 (M4)
Huber, H, F 431 (R3)
Hudson, O 092 (W4)
Hughes, H 824 (A3)
Hughes, S 421 (F4)
Hughes, G 543 (D6)
Hultberg, Eric, F 706 (B2)
Humbert, L, S 920 (F6)
Humphrey, L, H 436 (I5)
Hung, Bow, Thy 506 (H3)
Hunkin, S, A 958 (J4)
Hunrick, Geo 807 (J2)
Hunt, John 139 (O3)
Hunt, E, A 447 (R1)
Hunter, B, D 368 (K4)
Hunter, Lumber 980 (O1)
Hurley, Mrs, D, J 286 (N5)
Hurll, W, F 173 (G5)
Husband, J, M 871 (B5)
Hussey, Mrs, E, B 607 (F3)
Hutchins, Fred 778 (O5)
Hutchinson, Mrs, C ... 773 (E5)
Hutton, Mrs, S 720 (P5)
Hyde, Mrs, K 089 (E4)

I

Iacono, Angelina 701 (K2)
Ianetta, Lawrence ... 219 (M3)
Ide, Allen, C 593 (E5)
Ihde, Fred, E 382 (F3)
Iles, Chas 398 (R1)
Illiano, Salvatore 930 (N2)
Imanaka, Wm 227 (F4)
Imbagliazzo, R 298 (P6)
Ingram, Rupert 561 (E6)
Inlow, Myles, S 650 (D4)
Inman, Ernest 118 (H3)
Inskeep, Jack 348 (G5)
Inskeep, Wm, K 211 (J5)
Irvin, Hazel, E 279 (P4)
Irwin, Mrs, Vava 280 (C1)

Isaac, Yohanan 781 (G6)
Isaacs, Saml 084 (J2)
Isaacson, L, E 290 (L2)
Isaacson, M, C 914 (M6)
Isbitz, Jos 057 (E6)
Isen, Julian 108 (G5)
Isenberg, Vern 255 (E1)
Iserson, Anita 055 (E4)
Isham, S, Wood 358 (N5)
Ivancich, Katie 968 (N1)
Ivelia, Jr, Jos 052 (D6)
Ivy, Mrs, Maggie, L ... 844 (Q4)
Izykowski, Louis 111 (G1)

J

Jackson, Wm 623 (G3)
Jackson, C, A 794 (G5)
Jackson, Mrs, E 425 (I3)
Jackson, Mrs, E 457 (L3)
Jacobs, Jos 063 (K5)
Jacobsen, Mrs, A 265 (E2)
Jacobsen, John, A 761 (M3)
Jacot, Mrs, H, G 092 (J6)
Jallu, V 278 (C3)
James, Mrs, L, H 755 (A3)
James, Walter, D 693 (H6)
James, Mrs, H 925 (H6)
James, Thomas 286 (M2)
James, Vernon, C 660 (R3)
James, L, B 842 (R5)
Jameson, J 047 (F6)
Jameson, Guy, B 617 (I3)
Jameson, Helen 349 (L4)
Jensen, Mrs, C 918 (Q6)
Jessup, J, J 976 (R4)
Jim, De 617 (Q5)
Jochem, P 300 (F6)
Joe, Quock 057 (C1)
Johannessen, R 475 (D2)
Johns, Frank 693 (E3)
Johnson, Mrs, A 416 (A5)
Johnson, Mrs, C 374 (M4)
Jones, Mrs, Grace 835 (L2)
Jones, F, W 966 (M2)
Jordan, Mrs, L, H 383 (I5)
Jordan, Jr, I 947 (O2)
Jorgensen, Miss, P 789 (G1)
Jorgensen, Alfred 121 (O2)
Joris, L, E 966 (A5)
Joseph, John 787 (R4)
Joseph, F, Fraga 873 (R6)
Josephs, H, A 521 (P3)

Jow, Chen 990 (L1)
Jue, Jut 595 (Q3)

K

Kaaven, G 070 (M2)
Kaelin, Joseph, B 495 (L2)
Kahrs, Mrs, L 842 (F2)
Kaltenbrum, J 652 (R3)
Kane, F, P 643 (Q2)
Kapp, S, S 733 (P6)
Katich, Martin 329 (C5)
Kawaguchi, M 065 (H4)
Keegan, Dr, Theo 214 (O6)
Kelley, Mrs, C, K 934 (M2)
Kelley, Henry, F 687 (R5)
Kellogg, W, B 162 (E3)
Kellogg, Ernie 285 (G2)
Kelly, A, S 844 (H2)
Kelly, Mrs, Frank, J ... 794 (H2)
Kelsey, A, B 611 (C3)
Kelsey, Mrs, J, E 938 (M4)
Kelso, W, H 567 (J3)
Kempf, Mrs, Adele 835 (K3)
Kendall, A 489 (L5)
Kennedy, Mabel 992 (C2)
Kennedy, Mrs, J, J 649 (M4)
Kennedy, Mrs, E 080 (R4)
Kenney, I 564 (P1)
Kenrick, M, R 540 (Q4)
Keon, John, M 374 (E1)
Kergan, Dr, John 230 (P4)
Kerns, N, T 220 (D4)
Kerr, J 919 (E4)
Kessing, G, M 742 (P4)
Keyes, Dr, Henry 413 (C6)
Keyes, E, E 277 (N6)
Keyser, R, E 268 (D5)
Kiee, J, H 381 (C2)
Kieley, J, F 711 (I2)
Kiimalehto, Geo 202 (E2)
Kinnicutt, B, T 153 (Q5)
Kipschild, Fred, W 845 (J5)
Kister, W 231 (L5)
Kitchener, B 421 (G3)
Kleeman, Dr, G, E 280 (D3)
Kleenmn, Dr, F 905 (G2)
Kleiner, B 233 (L4)
Klewish, Mrs, C 441 (Q4)
Klopfer, F, W 260 (P2)
Knabbe, D 515 (F6)
Knierim, Mrs, H 104 (D5)
Knudsen, Martin 121 (O3)

RESIDENTIAL DIRECTORY

Koehler, C, H.............157 (B3)
Koenig, Kroll.............994 (N5)
Koford, MD, H...........870 (L3)
Kogler, Jos, T.............581 (J3)
Kondo, Y...................193 (G4)
Kopot, A....................909 (F3)
Kormann, F, A...........406 (G6)
Koughau, J................372 (N6)
Kramer, B..................183 (F1)
Krauss, F, B...............370 (D2)
Kreider, Mrs, E, J......265 (C5)
Kreischer, O..............643 (I6)
Kreiss, Louis.............394 (D4)
Kretz, Mrs, A.............717 (F4)
Kroeger, Claus..........308 (P4)
Krohn, L....................091 (F6)
Krueckel, A...............958 (K3)
Kuebler, S.................388 (C6)
Kuhlken, F, J.............910 (Q6)
Kuhnle, Fred.............958 (K3)
Kuhnle, W.................099 (Q4)
Kunhardt, C..............766 (G6)
Kurl-Finke, H, A........154 (H6)
Kurney, Mrs, C..........762 (O6)
Kwoon, On, Wo.........297 (I2)

L

La Fleur, A, A............439 (R2)
La Plant, J, L.............880 (F4)
Lafferty, Eugene.......733 (D3)
Lap, Tong.................300 (Q2)
Larkey, Dr, A, D.........479 (N4)
Larkin, Mrs, E, B........530 (F1)
Larson, O..................976 (F3)
Lathom, W, N............896 (M3)
Laughlin, Mrs, S........830 (G6)
Lauridsen, P.............608 (F3)
Lavorel, Mrs, A..........198 (M4)
Lavorel, Eugene, T....202 (Q1)
Law, So, Ton.............200 (C2)
Lawrence, E..............119 (E6)
Lawrence, Mrs, L......242 (F2)
Lawson, H, B.............464 (N1)
Layer, Herman..........471 (R2)
Layne, Mrs, M, E.......310 (J2)
Layton, W, D.............850 (G1)
Le Chandler, S..........059 (C6)
Le Protti, Mrs, E........702 (Q4)
Leadley, Phebe, A......519 (H1)
Leary, M, F...............324 (O6)
LeBeuf, Andy............289 (M3)
LeClair, P.................871 (M5)

Lee, Tung..................594 (J5)
Lee, Chas, A..............210 (P4)
Leeks, Mrs, B, C........623 (E5)
Leete, Mrs, E............977 (F3)
Leggett, Mrs, O.........655 (P1)
Leigh, Mrs, A............600 (C1)
Leisz, Geo, W............574 (O5)
Leith, E....................454 (G1)
Lemkau, Henry.........618 (A5)
Lemont, Aline...........516 (P2)
Leonard, Jas.............448 (H3)
Leonard, D...............133 (R5)
Leong, Pong.............905 (A5)
Lepper, Dr, A............210 (H5)
Leslie, Ira................833 (H4)
Lester, A..................754 (D2)
Lester, P, E...............149 (E2)
Leung, Heo, H..........714 (R2)
Leveira, B, B.............593 (E3)
Levenson, Percy, W...487 (C3)
Levy, P, J.................055 (B6)
Lew, Young...............301 (F3)
Lewin, Mrs, D, H........921 (J4)
Lewis, Mrs, Emma, J..150 (A4)
Lewis, Grant.............372 (O1)
Li, King, L................850 (F3)
Li, L, P.....................920 (R3)
Libcey, A, H..............382 (I5)
Libby, Eugene...........902 (E4)
Lightfoot, Mrs, D.......193 (R4)
Lilienthal, J...............445 (I2)
Lilley, G, E................637 (F4)
Lim, Hong................685 (C1)
Limsky, I..................273 (E6)
Lincoln, Mrs, H, D......148 (H6)
Lindemer, M.............327 (E4)
Lindsley, Mrs, A, H.....449 (C1)
Lingard, S, H.............167 (F2)
Lippincott, J, O..........249 (M4)
Liston, J, J................290 (G6)
Little, Geo, W............479 (K3)
Littlefield, J, T...........392 (D1)
Littrell, Mrs, John......687 (Q2)
Long, E....................019 (D6)
Long, Thos, S............105 (P2)
Longhead, J, H..........342 (C2)
Longwell, S, R...........379 (D5)
Lorentzen, Chas........744 (L3)
Lorenzen, Carl..........971 (O3)
Losee, A, W..............280 (I2)
Lothrop, T................833 (F1)
Loughead, J..............669 (H5)

Louie, Lam...............839 (B3)
Louie, Wing..............622 (E6)
Love, Mrs, Wilma......678 (H4)
Love, J, W................598 (Q4)
Lupino, I..................103 (B2)

M

Macauley, J...............590 (D1)
MacCann, Mrs, J........306 (H6)
MacDermot, Mrs........480 (H1)
Macdonald, W, D.......079 (A2)
Macdonald, Mrs.........266 (E5)
MacGregor, J, R.........256 (J1)
Mack, Con................264 (R4)
Mackay, Walter.........076 (C6)
Mackie, Wm, P..........914 (I5)
Mackinson, W, C........865 (Q3)
MacMillan, Mrs.........175 (P5)
Macnab, H................961 (G2)
Macomber, W...........677 (M4)
Madden, T................572 (I6)
Madison, H, P...........286 (R3)
Man, Sing.................595 (D2)
Man, Tick.................788 (L4)
Markley, W, A............344 (G3)
Marks, M, H..............696 (I2)
Marlin, B, W..............687 (N3)
Marre, Philip.............490 (C2)
Marsh, Xeon, F..........626 (F6)
Marsh, C, M..............349 (J2)
Marsh, Mrs, M, A........872 (R4)
Marshall, M...............124 (C5)
Marshall, Mrs, J.........547 (M1)
Marston, E, C............461 (F1)
Martin, A..................130 (D1)
Martin, Mrs, A, K........275 (D2)
Martin, Ellis..............758 (G3)
Martin, Harry............366 (R4)
Maschio, John...........892 (Q6)
Mason, Mrs, J, H........732 (I4)
Mason, G..................533 (Q6)
Masten, MD, B, B.......811 (N4)
Masterson, Mrs..........189 (G2)
Matherson, C............764 (P6)
Mathews, W, J...........706 (G6)
Mathis, G, V.............970 (E4)
Matsunaga, K...........162 (K5)
Mattern, C, W...........282 (E2)
Matthews, G.............187 (F3)
Mattson, C...............763 (R4)
Maul, Cilia, C............187 (C2)
Mayama, B...............388 (A4)

RESIDENTIAL DIRECTORY

Maycock, W. E..........104 (F1)
Mayer, Saml.............184 (Q5)
Maynard, F..............483 (O5)
Mazeres, Chas.........264 (N2)
McAfee, B. J............166 (Q2)
McArthur, B. S.........357 (J4)
McBride, Mrs, J........071 (N4)
McBroom, F.............106 (M3)
McCabe, P. B...........819 (M1)
McCain, E. J............590 (P1)
McCall, A. P............439 (P1)
McCarthy, David......593 (E5)
McCaslin, Irving.......942 (I6)
McCaw, Mrs, A........416 (M1)
McClellan, Mrs.........553 (E2)
McClenegan, J.........649 (D3)
McCloud, Bert.........442 (G3)
McClure, J. M..........688 (C6)
McConnell, D. P.......518 (I5)
McCormick, C..........980 (C1)
McCourtney, A, I......730 (D2)
McCoy, Mrs, P. L......158 (Q4)
McCracken, Dr.........914 (N5)
McCubbin, Mrs........182 (H2)
McCulloch, E...........721 (H3)
McDaniel, Dr, A, C...653 (E4)
McDermott, John......749 (F2)
McDonald, M...........658 (Q3)
McDonnell, P...........973 (I6)
McElroy, Mrs, B, M...064 (K6)
McEvilly, C.............744 (P5)
McFarland, Mr.........878 (O3)
McFherson, S...........331 (C4)
McGill, Mrs, A.........644 (N4)
McGillis, D. J...........662 (G1)
McGovern, J. J.........147 (M3)
McGran, Mrs, S........206 (M2)
McGrew, P. L...........454 (G3)
McGuire, W............899 (C6)
McHenry, B. L..........425 (I3)
McJunkin, Mrs, B......134 (R1)
McKay, Mrs, L, P......419 (G4)
McKeon, J, T...........200 (H2)
McKim, O, S...........260 (F6)
McKinlay, Perkins.....488 (J5)
McKinnon, A, B........787 (A1)
McLaren, Mrs, J.......474 (F4)
McLaughlin, Mrs......300 (F6)
McLeod, M.............123 (H3)
McInnis, M, A..........603 (D1)
McMahon, P............400 (D3)
McMannis, T, J.........674 (G2)

McMillen, P. W.........945 (H6)
McNabb, L, T..........178 (G6)
McNair, Dr, F, H.......246 (M4)
McNally, J, E...........786 (A4)
McNear, Mrs, G........921 (E2)
McNiel, Mrs, Alice....471 (R6)
McNulty, J, M..........053 (A4)
McSorley, Mrs, B......653 (F5)
McTeague, H...........645 (F3)
McVey, John, I.........950 (I4)
Mead, A, J.............793 (E6)
Mead, Jennie, M.......283 (N3)
Meade, M, D...........699 (P1)
Meads, H, W..........973 (C3)
Mears, F, E............749 (H6)
Medau, H, O...........111 (D5)
Medo, F, J.............909 (G3)
Meek, E, B.............396 (C3)
Meese, Walter..........757 (Q5)
Megraw, George......740 (B3)
Meissner, E, D.........934 (I6)
Melde, A, A............871 (F6)
Mellana, C.............070 (K3)
Miller, Mrs, N, J.......075 (C5)
Miller, Miss, M.........066 (H4)
Miller, B................098 (I5)
Millien, Mrs, E, F......962 (E4)
Mills, Mrs, B, A........718 (F5)
Mills, Mrs, H...........705 (L3)
Milwan, Beth, M.......679 (F2)
Minali, John............688 (H2)
Mingham, Chas........747 (M3)
Mong, Yee, Pong.....468 (F1)
Montgomery, W, P....577 (M5)
Montigue, John, E....108 (G2)
Montjar, Jessie.........566 (E4)
Montjar, Vera, A.......850 (I6)
Montjoy, Lynn, H......199 (Q2)
Montoya, Alex..........333 (D1)
Montoya, Joe, E.......576 (O2)
Montrose, Harry.......116 (F6)
Mooar, Robt, J.........649 (R3)
Mooberry, Mary, C....333 (C6)
Mood, E, E.............683 (P3)
Moodie, Mrs, B........199 (R1)
Moody, Burdett........467 (B2)
Moody, Walter, L......647 (C1)
Moody, Mrs, C.........750 (D5)
Moody, Elmer, I........164 (H1)
Moog, Camilla.........165 (G6)
Moohr, C...............180 (F3)
Moohr, Clara, M.......580 (M2)

Mook, Jennie...........288 (I6)
Moon, Peter............854 (C4)
Moon, Everett, C......194 (E3)
Moon, Bill..............666 (F6)
Moon, Webb...........384 (H2)
Moon, Spencer........389 (H2)
Moon, Harry, A........123 (J4)
Moone, Hiram, E......394 (H2)
Moone, Warner, S.....653 (M4)
Mooney, Douglas.....537 (P4)
Mooney, Ernest, W...146 (P6)
Moor, Weyert..........897 (G1)
Moorabian, Earl.......606 (Q6)
Mooradian, E..........947 (L2)
Moore, Bernard, J.....497 (B1)
Moore, Austin..........689 (F2)
Moore, Beatrice.......149 (O5)
Moore, Bernie..........277 (Q5)
Moore, Alfred, J.......791 (Q6)
Moorehead, Mrs.......095 (L6)
Moose, Loyal...........073 (D4)
Moran, J, T............402 (G4)
Morehouse, E, J.......974 (B5)
Morgan, M.............390 (G1)
Morodomi, S...........370 (K2)
Morrill, E, H............271 (A4)
Morris, Mrs, C, B......369 (G5)
Morris, W, T............610 (H4)
Morrison, Bev..........255 (N2)
Muller, Dr, O, J........577 (H5)
Muller, Yee............382 (I1)
Mullins, Mrs, K........523 (G3)
Munro, Alice...........071 (L3)
Munro, J, A............867 (C6)
Munson, H, F..........914 (C1)
Murdock, G............553 (R3)
Murphy, Mrs, A........940 (F5)
Murphy, D, H..........546 (M5)
Murphy, Robt, W......066 (N5)
Murray, C, M..........457 (E5)
Murray, Mrs, M........588 (Q6)
Muzzie, Joe............015 (L4)

N

Nahan, Mrs, M.........947 (O4)
Nakahara, K............087 (Q2)
Nanrungs, Mrs, E......609 (G6)
Nash, Mrs, I, W........562 (E2)
Nash, H................788 (G4)
Nathan, Mrs, J.........170 (F4)
Nathan, Miss, R........492 (I2)
Nead, J, M.............533 (J2)

RESIDENTIAL DIRECTORY

Neail, I 541 (C5)
Neddie, C.....................018 (Q1)
Needham, R, A 088 (I3)
Neff, Margaret, D 231 (Q2)
Nellist, Mrs, D, M...183 (R6)
Nelson, Capt, A.........720 (D1)
Nelson, Mrs, T............161 (G6)
Nelson, Julius.............960 (K3)
Nethercott, C, J.........825 (L3)
Netherland, Mrs, ...173 (Q4)
Neuvohner, S 989 (P2)
Newhall, O, G 897 (C6)
Newman, Mrs............996 (E3)
Neylan, Mrs, John 576 (A2)
Ngon, Yok..................754 (O3)
Nicely, O, M 643 (L3)
Nichols, Leslie, L 262 (N5)
Nichols, Mrs, O.........724 (Q4)
Nickel, Karl, H 554 (J2)
Niederstrasse 136 (N6)
Nielsen, Taylor, M...186 (C1)
Nielsen, C, S.............353 (G3)
Niemi, O 338 (I6)
Nishwitz, Mrs, J 272 (Q6)
Nissen, Miss, M........540 (R3)
Noble, A, P 197 (G5)
Noe, W, H..................431 (K4)
Nolan, D....................847 (J4)

O

O'Brien, Wm, H 106 (G5)
O'Connell, Mrs 511 (F4)
O'Connor, John..........961 (O5)
O'Farrell, J, G............052 (M1)
O'Grady, T, P 697 (P4)
O'Malley, D, J 689 (J4)
Ober, Wm 959 (G4)
Oberlies, M, Li...........540 (B3)
Ogden, Dr, Fred, S.....892 (R2)
Ohman, Oscar, T......356 (P6)
Okada, T....................595 (D1)
Old, Pineus 927 (H3)
Oliveira, P, J 566 (H3)
Oliver, Sarah.............776 (F1)
Ollis, Chas, B 965 (D3)
Olney, Wyatt.............994 (G2)
Olsen, Mrs, P.............909 (I1)
Olsen, Alex................787 (O2)
Olver, A, E 672 (F6)
One, Pred 578 (I2)
Onstott, C...................764 (J4)
Orem, Mrs, E, H........733 (G2)

Ormsby, M, P..............152 (C1)
Ortman, S 402 (C3)
Osgood, C, H.............402 (H5)
Otero, A, G 490 (B2)
Overfield, Jack...........145 (C6)
Overland, Merritt.......342 (Q2)
Oxley, Mrs, E, J 194 (F6)
Oy, Din, Tong 412 (F2)
Oyania, C..................651 (A5)

P

Pappageorge, H........390 (M6)
Paraschis, P...............153 (A5)
Parente, M.................439 (M2)
Park, Ed, L 363 (C6)
Parke, J, H 410 (F6)
Parker, Jos, J 368 (E2)
Parker, Miss, E 967 (E6)
Parker, N...................553 (K4)
Parkhurst, A, G.........779 (C3)
Parkinson, M.............780 (J4)
Parks, Donald 449 (G2)
Parrish, W H, D.........833 (K5)
Parsons, Mrs, A, S....311 (K6)
Parsons, B, B 092 (L1)
Partridge, Geo, H......605 (G2)
Pasaur, Mrs, S, I........766 (P2)
Paterasn, Dr, E, M 369 (C6)
Patrick, J, T 671 (J3)
Patterson, Dr, E, M ...330 (N1)
Paul, Lee, W 483 (O4)
Paulas, Angelo...........371 (Q1)
Paulding, B, M 532 (A2)
Paulding, Mrs, R, L ...074 (B5)
Paule, John, G...........381 (E1)
Paule, John................395 (O6)
Paules, Earl, G..........899 (K4)
Paules, Paul, B 899 (L2)
Pauley, Mrs, P...........918 (A3)
Pauley, Mary, E 977 (Q3)
Pauli, Frank, F 229 (N3)
Pauli, George, W 256 (Q2)
Pauli, Mrs, Richd.......908 (Q2)
Paulin, Cecile, J 161 (D2)
Paulin, Helen, M 066 (D3)
Paulin, Wallace 978 (N3)
Pauling, Linus 284 (H1)
Pauling, Mrs, A..........538 (P5)
Paulsen, Mrs, Dora....453 (D5)
Paulson, Saml 338 (Q2)
Paulus, C, D 242 (B4)
Paulus, Christopher...494 (J2)

Perez, P, J...................966 (K4)

Q

Quackenboss, C........178 (Q5)
Qualls, Lloyd, F 829 (B3)
Quamma, N 273 (F4)
Quick, David..............417 (K4)
Quick, Richd..............381 (K5)
Quiggle, Marjorie......771 (F2)
Quinlan, Frank, J 169 (Q6)
Quinn, Mrs, Bell 916 (F4)
Quinney, Lorraine 589 (D5)
Quintana, Maz...........567 (N5)
Quinton, Hubert 755 (A3)
Quinzell, Mrs..............929 (H2)
Quiring, Thos, C........769 (A2)
Quitzow, Roy.............788 (H6)

R

Ra, Florence 901 (N5)
Rach, Lewis, C 585 (P2)
Rampton, Jane 676 (Q4)
Ramsey, Robt 281 (C6)
Rath, John, C.............640 (R4)
Rathbone, Robt 281 (C6)
Rathbone, Mrs B710 (G3)
Rathbone, F, M 676 (Q4)
Rathbun, Miss, L.......139 (H1)
Rathbun, Jay, W 781 (M2)
Rathbun, Miss, L.......870 (M5)
Rathbun, Albt, S........309 (O1)
Rathbun, Ted, B.........465 (Q5)
Rathe, Henry 629 (M4)
Rather, Barney 373 (G2)
Rathlisberger, C 333 (H1)
Rathman, Geo, H......574 (E3)
Rathwell, T................413 (B4)
Rathwell, Thos, R 970 (J5)
Ratigan, James, P......331 (H4)
Ratigan, Thos 964 (P6)
Ratlae, E, N 140 (C3)
Ratzer, Minette..........155 (N6)
Ratzloff, Mrs, E 500 (P6)
Rau, Max, A 337 (E4)
Rau, Harry, W 782 (I1)
Raub, Mrs, Jack.........582 (F1)
Raub, Mrs, H.............130 (R5)
Raubes, Olawes, L 297 (F4)
Rauch, Marcus 945 (B3)
Rauch, Dwight 846 (B5)
Rauch, Lee 535 (G2)
Rauchfuss, G, R 127 (I2)

RESIDENTIAL DIRECTORY

Raucourt, Jules 508 (K5)
Rauen, Edward, F 496 (L3)
Rauer, Richd, J 673 (G3)
Raulerson, Bert, R 874 (O6)
Raulin, Paul, E 758 (F1)
Raulli, Raplh 354 (R4)
Raulston, Burrell, O ..701 (F2)
Raulston, Mrs, J, L 710 (I3)
Rauchfuss, G, R 127 (I2)
Raucourt, Jules 508 (K5)
Rauen, Edward, F 496 (L3)
Rauer, Richd, J 673 (G3)
Raulerson, Bert, R 874 (O6)
Raulin, Paul, E 758 (F1)
Raulli, Raplh 354 (R4)
Raulston, Burrell, O ..701 (F2)
Raulston, Mrs, J, L 710 (I3)
Redburn, Bradley, T ...139 (H1)
Reed, Srg., E 309 (O1)
Reich, Thos 964 (P6)
Rhimer, Ashley, E 465 (Q5)
Rhodes, Max, A 337 (E4)
Richards, Forrest, L ...297 (F4)
Rigg, Barney 373 (G2)
Riley, Mrs, L, M 582 (F1)
Robarts, Marcus 945 (B3)
Rockwell, Ralph 354 (R4)
Rooney, Jay, W 781 (M2)
Rose, C, ...232 (E1)
Rosen, Levi 304 (K5)
Ross, Agnes, ...014 (R3)
Ross, Mrs, Edith 500 (P6)
Rowan, Edward, F 496 (L3)
Rowe, Mrs, Betty, T ...130 (R5)
Rufton, Thomas, R 413 (B4)
Russel, Lee 535 (G2)
Ryder, Harry, W 782 (I1)

S

Sainty, Louis, E 703 (J5)
Saisoon, Wong 065 (G6)
Saiter, Mrs, Emma 946 (G5)
Saitman, Saml 208 (M3)
Saito, Mrs, H. 940 (E6)
Saito, Frank, K 317 (L4)
Slabaugh, Coeva 906 (G6)
Slack, Gertrude. 648 (E4)
Slack, Mrs, F, D 889 (J3)
Sladek, Mrs, E. 905 (M5)
Slader, Henry, L 855 (R6)
Sladovich, Milo 387 (H2)
Slaff, Chas 159 (E5)

Slaff, Leonard, I 537 (R4)
Slager, Emma, M 134 (E2)
Slagerman, B, V 181 (R6)
Slater, Mrs, Lillian 488 (A1)
Slater, James, A. 959 (C1)
Slater, Isador 099 (L1)
St Jean, Ray 169 (J3)
St Jean, Mrs, J, E 669 (P6)
St John, Valentine 936 (R4)
St Lawrence, L, G 680 (N2)
St Pierre, AJ 949 (M3)
St Pierre, Mabel 569 (R3)
Stein, Mrs, Trudy 012 (M4)
Svendsen, E, G 690 (P3)
Svenson, H 552 (D4)
Svenson, Arthur 852 (F1)
Svensson, Robt, H. 496 (N1)
Sverdrup, H. 938 (H1)
Sverdrup, Harold, U ...987 (O1)
Svoboda, Marie 633 (A3)
Svolos, Nick 155 (K4)
Swab, Alexander 734 (B3)
Swaboda, Gustav 679 (Q1)
Swacker, E, W 400 (E4)
Swader, Richd 828 (M2)
Swadffield, R, G 186 (O4)
Swagler, Ralph 852 (I5)
Swagler, Ralph 801 (J6)
Swaim, Estelle 525 (E4)
Swain, Mrs, Fred. 091 (G2)
Swan, Aleck, M 606 (C1)
Swan, Fletcher, J 930 (H3)
Swan, Victor 516 (A5)
Swan, Virginia 225 (B7)
Swanberg, Geo 106 (C1)
Swanbom, Karl 764 (I2)
Swanburg, F 086 (F2)
Swanburg, Mabel 213 (H1)
Swanby, H. 180 (F1)

T

Tabak, Michl 134 (D2)
Tabb, Anges. 907 (N2)
Tabron, Mrs, M. 326 (F2)
Tacono, John 561 (K3)
Tafoya, Chas, P 156 (I3)
Tafoya, Anna 048 (K3)
Taggart, Mrs, M. 634 (N5)
Tagunov, Leonard, J ..409 (J3)
Taipale, Eliz, R 713 (H3)
Tait, T, Cliff 869 (K4)
Tait, Adam. 772 (P2)

Talbert, Mary 433 (F6)
Talbot, Jas, E 330 (K6)
Talbott, Lola 735 (M6)
Talley, G, C 976 (F4)
Tallish, Charlotte 957 (D6)
Tallman, C, B. 333 (G2)
Tallman, Lucy. 534 (N4)
Tally, Walter 442 (N2)
Talmadge, T, B 635 (E4)
Tamble, Geo, E 920 (K2)
Tamburich, V. 782 (E1)
Tammi, Jack, J 961 (Q1)
Tangye, Mrs, C 091 (D5)
Tankie, Antone, P 104 (D2)
Tannehill, Earl, E 463 (D2)
Tanner, W, P 111 (G5)
Tanner, Floyd 257 (N3)
Tanney, Ray 798 (O5)
Tantardino, V 124 (F3)
Taormina, C, V 850 (C1)
Taormina, A, D 440 (P1)
Tapia, Mrs, Adella 962 (H6)
Tapia, Juana, P 256 (M4)
Taplin, Irvin, C 595 (M3)
Tarango, Jesus 990 (L4)
Tarango, Frank 942 (R2)
Tarbet, Claude 722 (D3)
Tarin, Henry 425 (R4)
Tarney, Donald, O 397 (A5)
Taros, Nick 592 (B4)
Tarr, Lewis, R 183 (G4)
Taslo, Fabian 375 (I3)
Tassey, Chas, M 847 (K5)
Tassey, Mary, L. 557 (L3)
Tassio, S, John 429 (H4)
Tate, Henry, E 441 (H5)
Taucher, M. 676 (M3)
Taunt, Marie, N 939 (B4)
Tavenor, Wm, J. 713 (N4)
Taylor, C, A 538 (D5)
Taylor, Danl, D 938 (H2)
Taylor, Herbt, T 460 (J6)
Tebow, June 825 (L1)
Tedd, Clifford 275 (J2)
Tedder, Chas, W 704 (J4)
Tedesco, Frank 310 (O5)
Teel, Valerie 978 (D1)
Teepe, John 202 (B3)
Teeters, Mrs, Lee. 241 (G4)
Teets, Robt. 442 (H5)
Teget, Bruce, O. 859 (K4)
Tekin, Agnes. 366 (M3)

RESIDENTIAL DIRECTORY

Telesford, I, Rubio 884 (G1)
Tellefsen, J..................254 (J6)
Teller, Wm 276 (F2)
Telles, Hazel................229 (N4)
Temblador, Frank 074 (E3)
Temblador, Jackie 604 (R5)
Temme, Chas..............653 (J4)
Tempe, Carl, R............718 (L1)
Templeman, R............114 (C1)
Templeton, Mrs,..........507 (E5)
Templeton, H, B..........681 (F5)
Tennant, John, J 920 (C3)
Teoli, Vincent..............531 (O2)
Teoli, Carmen..............100 (P4)
Terry, Alf, L..................469 (K2)
Tessier, Harvey 273 (Q5)
Teters, Irwin................325 (L1)
Teuber, Rolf, F............648 (H2)
Tew, Mrs, Ella 211 (D5)
Tewso, Fred 171 (F6)
Thacker, Robt, C........895 (A5)
Thalia, Ardrell............108 (P2)
Tharp, Betty 796 (E3)
Tharp, Florence..........937 (L5)
Thayer, Anne..............574 (E5)
Thayer, O, C 304 (M2)
Thebeau, B..................720 (M4)
Theilen, Iona..............388 (D1)
Thermos, Peter 257 (H3)
Theye, G, L 254 (F4)
Thibado, Eldon, J 792 (A1)
Thiele, Edw, C............436 (D6)
Thien, Vernon, J 183 (B6)
Thigpen, A..................650 (B5)
Thigpen, Joel, W 744 (D2)
Thivus, Theofanis 221 (B3)
Thobois, Juliette 857 (E4)
Thomas, Mrs, C 487 (D3)
Thomas, Dilbert 996 (I2)
Thomasgaard, N 385 (H4)
Thomason, B, O 084 (E4)
Thomason, C, O 686 (J6)
Thomley, Ralph, M....552 (A3)
Thompson, Margt 150 (K3)
Thompson, Mrs, G....507 (M6)
Thompson, L..............718 (N3)
Thor, Arth..................673 (B5)
Thorington, R..............439 (D4)
Thornburg, R 491 (Q3)
Thornton, Betty 288 (H5)
Thorp, Ella, A 423 (B6)
Thorpe, Della 150 (F4)

Thorsell, Hugo............758 (Q6)
Thrapp, Helene..........361 (C4)
Thresher, Alf, W 053 (G2)
Thues, Luther..............998 (K3)
Thurman, M................452 (G2)
Thurston, D 895 (D1)
Thuss, John 270 (P5)
Thweatt, Silas, A 489 (R4)
Tiabado, E, J 466 (F2)
Tibbens, David, L......726 (Q4)
Tibbs, Mrs, P, K..........178 (G5)
Tico, Wm, R................887 (D5)
Tidwell, Mrs, M,........668 (N6)
Tiebout, Ralph............829 (P2)
Tietz, Jos, M..............297 (N1)
Tilley, Chas, L............615 (F1)
Tillie, Mry..................345 (N3)
Tillman, Wm 400 (E2)
Tillman, Lilly..............132 (M3)
Timbrook, Chas, E 739 (B5)
Timmer, John, W 475 (R2)
Timms, Aug, G............562 (A1)
Tindall, Walter............843 (B1)
Tinkler, Harold 641 (F2)
Tinney, Jay................321 (L1)
Tipich, Martin, V........885 (E4)
Tisdale, Clay, S..........949 (F3)
Titchener, Edw, J........225 (D4)
Tittle, Robt 275 (Q6)
Titze, Louise 919 (G1)
Toberman, Homer 106 (R3)
Tobias, Vos................134 (R6)
Todd, John, K............229 (M1)
Tolentino, Ignacio 655 (E5)
Tollefsen, Mae............762 (H3)
Toman, Minnie 795 (C2)
Tomasello, Mrs, T 264 (D4)
Tomich, Nina 317 (M1)
Tooker, Dwain 777 (H1)
Toole, Mary 647 (K4)
Tope, Mrs, Margt 380 (P2)
Torplund, Edwin, R 546 (L2)
Torrance, Mureal 131 (I6)
Torre, Jos, F................916 (F1)
Torres, Marcelino 093 (D3)
Torres, Rafaelita........972 (Q3)
Torstorm, Olaf, G......942 (M2)
Tortarolo, Nicola......469 (F1)
Toupin, LeRoy, P........230 (G3)
Tousseau, Melvin......601 (M5)
Townshed, C, C 096 (F3)
Tracey, Wm, H 516 (K5)

Tracy, Chris, C............054 (N4)
Trammell, C................199 (F1)
Trampus, Wm, H 495 (J4)
Trani, Frank 330 (K6)
Trautz, Oscar, J 611 (E3)
Trefethen, N................112 (R3)
Treff, John, P..............329 (E4)
Trejo, Mrs, Aselia 982 (E2)
Trent, Lawrence 800 (E5)
Triffon, Jas, A............540 (E3)
Trigg, John, J............069 (G6)
Tripsevich, Geo..........795 (O3)
Triunfo, Lillan............978 (J3)
Trousdale, Chas........249 (C1)
Trujilli, Mathilda........354 (G5)
Trumbly, C..................687 (P1)
Truscott, Anna..........784 (L1)
Truxler, Louise, X 994 (H2)
Tubbs, Burton, W 311 (G1)
Tuck, Austin, C..........994 (H2)
Tucker, E, B................471 (F6)
Turnbull, Septimus 086 (R5)
Turner, Doyle 568 (F2)
Tuttle, W, M................602 (A4)
Tweedy, Willis, W 364 (M6)
Twing, Mrs, Elsie 692 (F5)
Tyler, Stanley, S........950 (C5)
Tyler, Cornelius..........970 (D2)
Tyrrell, Joyce............436 (L5)
Tyson, Ida, L..............287 (G4)

U

Ugalde, R 753 (O3)
Uhlain, Eliz................359 (C3)
Ulery, Lee, H..............702 (B3)
Ulery, Laura, C..........760 (P4)
Ullman, Sofia, H 456 (N4)
Ullmer, Herbt, H........400 (G3)
Ullom, Marlyn............508 (B1)
Ulrich, Jas 237 (C1)
Ungaro, Ivan, G........673 (A4)
Urry, Stanley..............766 (G3)
Uruburu, Krono..........613 (R5)
Utovac, Matt, R........426 (A5)
Uusitalo, Paavo..........599 (H3)

V

Vagenas, Duane, L....688 (H4)
Valdez, Tino..............519 (P4)
Valdez, Celestino......691 (Q2)
Valera, Arturo............918 (L5)
Valley, L, L................309 (Q2)

RESIDENTIAL DIRECTORY

Van, Chas, W 776 (C2)	Welk, Osma, C...........323 (O3)	Wolff, Violet 764 (F2)
Vanderburg, P, S 565 (G6)	Welker, Mrs, Lillian....429 (A1)	Wood, Elmer, O 445 (C2)
Vanderhoof, Mrs, F....534 (O2)	Welker, Walter, F.......279 (G5)	Wood, S, D.................965 (G6)
Vanderpool, P, S 236 (G2)	Well, Rebecca............658 (A5)	Wood, Wm, W 378 (H2)
Vanderwoort, P 115 (E5)	Well, Hildon...............653 (Q2)	Wood, Kenyon 413 (O4)
Vandette, David 815 (C4)	Welland, Roy 643 (C6)	Woodall, W, H 257 (D4)
VanHouten, J 426 (C2)	Welland, Miss, L.........087 (Q1)	Woodard, Fred, C 973 (I5)
Vaughan, L, C 197 (D6)	Welland, Mrs, A, ...643 (Q3)	Woodbury, Benj, R 177 (Q2)
Veeck, Bertha............511 (J4)	Wellborn, Jr, Olin 859 (F1)	Woodford, Mrs, E......342 (F3)
Veit, Louise 970 (J3)	Wellborn, Annie, B 458 (H3)	Woodhouse, Roy 832 (R4)
Ventura, S 211 (L3)	Wellborn, Mrs, Ch.....544 (H4)	Woodman, A...............637 (G2)
Verenkoff, Peter.........191 (N6)	Wellbrock, H M 724 (A3)	Woodruff, Gerald 630 (Q1)
Verila, Dick 611 (G6)	Wellck, Walter, F.......324 (C1)	Woods, C, F...............051 (K2)
Vidano, Peter............828 (J3)	Wellemeyer, L 184 (F3)	Woodson, Carl, O 488 (M2)
Vidovich, G................922 (A2)	Weller, Dana, R.........873 (D5)	Woodworth, W 965 (P3)
Vidovich, Mike...........241 (N6)	Wells, Leonard 804 (A1)	Workman, Max 146 (R4)
Vidovich, D................964 (P2)	Wells, Rebecca..........886 (Q1)	Wren, Ernest..............535 (O3)
Vigil, Manuel 812 (A3)	Wendell, Paul, P.........323 (G5)	Wright, A, S...............751 (C3)
Vigil, Flavio 115 (I2)	Werner, Birdie, A 863 (Q5)	Wright, Noel 127 (E2)
Villa, V, C 746 (H2)	Wert, Mavin, O 691 (R2)	Wright, L, LeeRoy.....724 (F2)
Vincent, Mrs, N...........508 (A1)	Wesa, Mrs, Anna.......184 (B3)	Wymore, Glenn, A 512 (G4)
Vincenza, Sam...........528 (G4)	Wesson, Lola, M.........120 (K2)	
Vines, Roxy 664 (R3)	West, Bjarne, W.........321 (C3)	**X**
Vinko, Morris.............590 (G6)	West, Hayward, E 876 (C5)	
Vinson, Leslie, C 527 (B2)	Wettenbarger, C........763 (M4)	Xitco, Anna................105 (E3)
Virga, Rose, M 284 (F1)	Wheat, Ted, M 940 (A5)	Xitco, John, J.............497 (O1)
Virta, Oscar, J............096 (G6)	Whedon, Edwin, F.......942 (C2)	Xitco, Mary................787 (P2)
Viskovich, Steven 668 (C6)	Wheeler, Mrs, P..........279 (A4)	
Viskovich, Alex 403 (O4)	Wheeler, Orville..........386 (K4)	**Y**
Viskovich, Vincent 125 (Q2)	Wheeler, Newman 490 (O4)	
Vitale, Anthony 731 (D1)	Whitaker, Jerome 983 (R2)	Yates, E, Alvin 255 (G4)
Vix, Theo...................704 (F6)	White, Theil, E...........976 (G1)	Yerkov, Nick 207 (D1)
Vladick, Anthony........365 (F1)	White, Bernard...........563 (K1)	York, Mrs, Stella 780 (G5)
Von, Aspe, Elsa 817 (G4)	White, Jerry 244 (K2)	Young, Robt, G 504 (C2)
Voorhees, Chas, H 076 (R4)	White, Delmon 934 (P5)	Young, Walter, L........748 (G5)
Voss, Anna, M............200 (M5)	White, Wayne 999 (Q1)	Young, Axel 623 (P3)
	Whitford, Doris 725 (P5)	Young, Leslie, A.........806 (R6)
W	Wick, John 250 (P5)	Younge, Ruth 733 (F2)
Warner , Leov............992 (D1)	Wiese, Jesse, C..........735 (F3)	**Z**
Watt , Lorene.............486 (B7)	Wilburn, Mrs, U..........994 (E5)	
Watters , Lorraine.....436 (C5)	Wilcox, Percy.............050 (G4)	Zabica, Marco...........250 (K6)
Webb, O 299 (I4)	Williams, Edna 374 (D4)	Zalman, Lyle, P...........273 (C6)
Weber, Margaret 812 (K6)	Williams, C, A 841 (F3)	Zander, Eva, F...........427 (I5)
Welch, Mrs, Pearl 397 (D4)	Williams, Jasper 110 (Q3)	Zaninovich, Tony.......297 (Q2)
Welch , Mattie...........873 (A1)	Wilson, Billie 472 (A5)	Zankich, Andw, J 151 (Q2)
Welch , Mary.............114 (C3)	Wilson, X, U...............849 (C3)	Zar, Nick...................588 (O3)
Welch , Marjorie.........48 (O1)	Wilson, Lamen, H.......825 (Q2)	Zarro, Geo 669 (H5)
Weld, Arthur, E 551 (D5)	Winchester, F, W.........565 (P2)	Zimmer, David...........875 (E1)
Weld, Max, L.............395 (F3)	Wing, Jacque, C.........074 (B3)	Zimmer, Ofa 723 (K2)
Welday, Mrs, M 242 (J2)	Wise, Renee, R...........956 (I2)	Zimmmerman, N.......254 (P6)
Welfer, Harry.............673 (Q6)	Wolf, R, Don..............423 (J6)	Zink, Albt, H 651 (L6)
Welk, Herman, R 798 (J5)	Wolfe, Walter, G 160 (R6)	Zorotovich, Phyllis, D 516 (P1)
		Zuanich, Marino, J....574 (C5)
		Zwart, Wm, C............611 (O2)

CHARACTER QUALITY

AMERICA!

ENTERPRISE ACCURACY

Los Angeles Standard

AN AMERICAN PAPER FOR THE AMERICAN PEOPLE

THE GREAT NEWSPAPER OF THE GREAT SOUTHWEST

CALIFORNIA FORECAST
Los Angeles and vicinity - Fair and mild Fr. and Sa. San Francisco and vicinity - Fair Fr! Sa. unsettled.

MEAN TEMPERATURES
Los Angeles 61
Seattle 42
New York 49
Chicago 38
New Orleans . . 74
Salt Lake 41

VOL. XLIII

THURSDAY MORNING, APRIL 1, 1948

DAILY, FIVE CENTS

RUSSIANS BACK DOWN IN BERLIN

TRYING TO LAND - USAF Flies 15,000 pounds of food into Berlin.

British Tanks and Troops Move on Control Post and Reds Decide to Get Out

BERLIN, (U.P.) – The Russians withdrew late last night from a control station they set up in the British sector of Berlin after 400 British troops, supported by nine armored cars, surrounded them on three sides.

The British victory in a new war of nerves came after a tense day during which the United States and British army chieftains defied a virtual Soviet blockade of Berlin by ordering their air forces to set up emergency service for passengers and freight between the capital and their occupation zones.

In addition to demanding the right to inspect all Allied railroad and transport moving between Berlin and the western occupation zones, the Russians for two hours set up roadblocks along the boundary of their zone in Berlin.

Tanks Move In

The Russians withdrew these posts. But near the Gatow Airfield the Russians suddenly established a control station in what the British said was their area.

First five light British tanks moved to the scene. They were withdrawn later. But 400 troops with their armored cars moved in. They maneuvered into position so as to cut the Russians off on three sides. The only path open to the Russians was a direct line of retreat into their own quarter. There were about 20 Russians, including six officers, at the station.

Both groups remained grimy alert while the British commandant demanded that the Russians withdrew and the Russians refused to do so without orders from their high command.

Change of Mind?

Whether they got these orders, or merely changed their minds when they saw the Tommies around them, was not immediately known.

In any event, the British command announced, the Russians withdrew in an orderly fashion and without incident just before midnight.

The British action was the first effective retort to the new Russian nerve war.

Flatly rejecting a Russian demand to inspect railroad trains between Berlin and the Western occupation zones, the American and British commanders in chief canceled all their train services. Motor transport, also subject to Russian inspection, was curtailed.

Protest Rejected

Last night Lt. Gen. G. S. Lukyanchenko, Russian chief of staff, rejected a new protest against the Red army blockade made by Maj. Gen. Nevil Brownjohn, British deputy commander in chief, on behalf of himself and his western allies.

The crisis caused by the Russian demand to the right of inspecting Allied transport was intensified when the Red army established its blockade on the boundaries of its zone inside the capital.

This blockade was called off after two hours but later the Russian command announced that no motor transport would be permitted to move into, out of, or inside the Russian quarter of the city between 11 p.m. And 6 a.m.

U.S. Flies in Food

American headquarters announced that two transport planes had brought in 15,000 pounds of food in the first fulfillment of Gen. Lucius D. Clay's promise that United States troops and civilians here would be fully supplied by plane.

At the same time, unofficial reports said that the Russians had let a German-operated train carrying supplies from the American port of Bremerhaven enter the city without incident after only a routine check.

NEWSPAPER

Beach Crowd Enjoys Sun; Rain Still Due

Intermittent rain was forecast for today by the U.S. Weather Bureau yesterday while a crowd of more than 45,000 people basked in the spring sunshine at Santa Monica.

So vast was the throng of beach frolickers that extra life-guards were ordered to patrol the seashore at Santa Monica. Ideal surf conditions prevailed for spring vacationers, although the water temperature was a chilly 56 degrees.

A few showers tonight and tomorrow were predicted, following intermittent rain today. Snow is expected in mountain areas above 7000 feet today and 5000 feet tomorrow. It also will be cooler and locally windy, the weatherman said.

At Los Angeles Harbor a dense fog which paralyzed shipping movements yesterday morning forced four ships to anchor in the outer roadstead for four hours. Several sailings were jogged off schedule, too.

Haze and smoke shrouded the metropolitan area from 8:30 a.m. to 12:40 p.m., with a 30-mile visibility range at 7 a.m. reduced to 1 mile at 11 a.m. Temperature downtown ranged from 42 to 69 degrees.

Tommy Dorsey Weds Dancer in Deep South

ATLANTA – Band Leader Tommy Dorsey, the "sentimental gentleman of swing," was married here today to Jane New of New York, Copacabana dancer.

It was Dorsey's third marriage. Dorsey's second wife, Starlet Pat Dane, said she was shocked.

"It's a big shock," Pat said. "We've been talking almost every night and he was supposed to fly out here (Hollywood) Monday.

"I'm hurt because he didn't let me in on the secret."

The newlyweds will honeymoon briefly on his yacht in Miami before Dorsey's band goes on tour April 7.

Clara Rose Breathes Easy as Youth Arrested

Hollywood – Actress Clara Rose was interviewed on the set of her new film "Leopard People", finally addressing rumors that police were investigating a break-in at her home. Rose said that a youth was arrested by police for break-and-enter.

"I'm relieved the matter is settled," said the star. "Now surely there is other news to cover."

The incident occurred in February while Rose was abroad. A number of items including expensive perfumes, clothing, and jewelry were stolen. According to other sources, Miss Rose also received threatening letters, which may be why she is now living at a second residence.

LAPD Detective Henry McTeague issued a statement: "It is my opinion that Miss Rose was targeted after her home was featured in the December issue of Photoplay magazine. She has, however, decided not to press charges."

Anonymous tips led to the early morning arrest of a 17-year-old suspect, at his home. Due to the boy's age, he cannot be named, and is expected to be released into parental care later today.

The Detective wouldn't comment further about ongoing investigations, but anonymous sources suggest that the minor is also a suspect in at least two other break-ins in the wealthy neighborhood.

DRAFT MEASURE PROPOSED

Washington D.C. (U.P.) – Military leaders prepared to lay before Congress tomorrow a draft bill reportedly calling for the registration of all men between 18 and 45.

Defense Secretary Forrestal and Army Secretary Royall will go before the Senate Armed Services Committee to discuss the proposed draft and the defense plans, one of which calls for an added military budget of $10,000,000,000.

Defense officials said it is a "good educated guess" that Forrestal's draft measure will call for the registration of all men between the ages of 18 and 45. But only single men between 18 and 25 would be inducted.

Smoking Called Coronary Heart Disease Factor

Chicago (AP) – An article in the health magazine Hygeia said today that coronary thrombosis has increased sharply among women and that "smoking may have something to do" with it.

Coronary thrombosis is a form of heart disease caused by formation of a blood clot in one of the heart arteries. This condition blocks the blood supply to a portion of the heart.

Ratio Drops

Writing in Hygeia, published by the American Medical Association, Irene E. Soehren of The Dalles, said men once developed the condition from 50 to 60 times as frequently as women. Now, she added, one woman has the condition for every three men.

"Generally speaking, the reason that women have it less is that their metabolic systems take care of cholesterol better than men's . . .

"Recent medical opinion is that diet has much to do with the increase in coronary heart disease. People eat too much of animal fats, bacon, egg yolks, pie a la mode, gravy, cream, butter, fat meats. These foods produce an excess of cholesterol in the blood . . . When there is too much, plaques of cholesterol are laid down in the lining of the arteries, especially the coronary arteries. On these deposits the blood clot forms, blocking the artery, and one has a thrombosis."

Tests at Mayo Clinic

She said tests conducted at Mayo Clinic on four groups of 1000 patients each indicated that "on the average, smokers were found to get coronary thrombosis 10 years earlier than non-smokers."

"Although not a cause of the disease, smoking is considered by many cardiologists to be a factor," she stated.

She said the disease is "not a death sentence," and that "many patients go back to so nearly normal that one cannot tell they have had a coronary attack."

GLOBAL DETECTIVE AGENCY TO TAKE OVER FOR TROUBLED POLICE DEPARTMENT

Private Investigation firm retained after Scandal, Suspension of Chief of Police

The Global Detective Agency (GDA) – a private investigation firm, will continue to conduct investigations in Los Angeles under mandate from the California District Attorney, Walter G. Sampson, while the Police Department copes with the ongoing ramifications of last year's "Grim Sunday" scandal.

Putting the investigation of felony crimes in the hands of a private agency is an unprecedented step that underscores the extent to which scandal has rattled the foundations of local law enforcement. The decision comes as a result of a Grand Jury recommendation that the city appoint an independent body to investigate major crimes until the public trust in the police department can be restored.

GDA personnel are licensed to carry weapons and conduct investigations. They will now be empowered to enter active crime scenes, question police witnesses, and investigate evidence.

"The Global Detective Agency is a professional, highly efficient private investigation firm with branches throughout the United States," said District Attorney Sampson. "I have full confidence in their ability to enforce the law while I continue to work with the Mayor and FBI to rebuild the department. I recognize that this is not an ideal situation for anyone, but I give you my word that every opportunity will be made to rebuild the Los Angeles Police Department into a trustworthy body which can be depended upon to abide by, and enforce, the laws of the State of California."

Decision to transfer investigations to the GDA was the result of a recent county grand jury investigation into the "Grim Sunday" case which uncovered rampant abuses in the major crimes division. The unfolding scandal led to the indictments of 12 officers and the suspension of dozens more including James Maloney, the Chief of Police.

RIDEOUT JOINS THE RACE FOR SHALLENHOCK'S TOWN

HOLLYWOOD – It has been quite the year so far, for Los Angeles Mayor Arthur Shallenhock and his city council. With half a dozen city councilors facing charges of corruption, money laundering, and tax evasion, and a police force all but decimated by the recent Grim Sunday scandal, one might think that campaigning for re-election in such a climate would be an uphill battle.

In classic Shallenhock style, however, the much-loved, charismatic mayor has seemed like he's been a hundred places at once – kissing babies and cutting ribbons – as the countdown to official campaign season begins. Just last Tuesday, Shallenhock – a well-known dart-enthusiast – played the parts of both Master of Ceremonies and winner of the competition at the Los Angeles Rotary Club's annual Charity Dart-a-thon.

Meanwhile, there are already signs that the mayoral race may not prove quite as simple for Shallenhock and his team this time around. A few of his recent appearances, including last weekend's Venice Beach Pig-Roast, have been marred by vocal protestors insisting the mayor himself be held accountable for the corruption in the police force and City Hall.

And now it looks like he's got other things to worry about. Yesterday, in a surprise announcement, local businessman Bradley Rideout held a press conference to declare his candidacy for Mayor of Los Angeles.

Up until now, Shallenhock has had no credible opposition. Though by no means as high-profile as the former radio and television personality Shallenhock, Rideout is a man of some respect, and his message of running for the common man, not the Hollywood movie-star seems to be striking a chord with possible voters.

"Do we really need more glitz, more glamour, more tinsel in Tinseltown?" asked Rideout to a packed house at the Avoy Social Club. "Do we need more fakery, more fairytales, more la-la in La-La-Land? I say no! What we need is more food on the table, more gas in the tank, and more accountability at City Hall." It appears to be a message that is resonating with some citizens.

Rideout's critics, meanwhile, are already questioning some of his businesses ties to certain Los Angeles crime syndicates. In fact, one reporter at the press conference asked about this specifically.

"My friend is the common man," answered Rideout, "wherever he may be".

Could it be our shiny Shallenhock has finally met his match?

Today Radio Programs

Thursday, April 1.

- AS PROVIDED BY STATIONS -

		KDKA – 1020 NBC Red Network	WCAE – 1250 Mutual Network	WJAS – 1320 Columbia Network	KQV – 1410 Blue Network
4	PM	Backstage Wife -sketch	News	Music	Club Matinee
	:15	Stella Dallas – sketch	Tune Factory	Green Valley Usa	News
	:30	Lorenzo Jones – sketch	Continued	Health Highways	Club Matinee
	:45	Widder Brown – sketch	Continued	Mickey Ross Orch.	Music: News
5	PM	A Girl Marries – sketch	News: Tune Factory	Mickey Ross Orch.	Melody Parade
	:15	Portia Faces Life – sk.	Tune Factory	Mother and Dad	Continued
	:30	Just Pain Bill – sk.	Continued	Are you a Genius	Jack Armstrong – sk.
	:45	Front Page Farrell – sk.	Continued	Ben Bernie – music	Captain Midnight
6	PM	News: Music	Baron Elliott Orch.	Frazier Hunt – news	Terry and The Pirates
	:15	Dinner Date	News	Beckler Smith – news	Sports
	:30	Songs for Soldiers	Foreign News	John B. Kennedy – ne.	News
	:45	Lowell Thomas – news	Uncle Sam	World Today – news	Modernaires
7	PM	Fred Waring Orch.	Filnton Lews – news	Amos 'n' Andy- Com.	Those Good Old Days
	:15	John Vandercook – Ne.	Franklen Masters Orch.	Harry James Orch.	Continued
	:30	Bob Burns	Confidentially Yours	Easy Aces	Metropolitan Op. USA
	:45	Continued	News	Mr. Keen	Continued
8	PM	Frank Morgan	Singin' Sam	Meet Corliss Archer	Earl Godwin – news
	:15	(And Fannie Brice)	Music	Continued	Lum and Abner
	:30	Aldrich Family	Dark Destiny	Death Valley	Town Meeting
	:45	Continued	Continued	Continued	Continued
9	PM	Bing Crosby Hour	Gabriel Heatter – news	Major Bowes Amateurs	Town Meeting
	:15	Continued	"Impact" – drama	Continued	Continued
	:30	Rudy Vallee	Treasury of Song	Stage Door Canteen	Spotlight Bands
	:45	Continued	Continued	Continued	Continued
10	PM	Abbott and Costello	NRav Clapper	"First Line" – navy	Ravm. G. Swing-news
	:15	Continued	Brazil Presents	Continued	Gracie Fields
	:30	March of Time	Camp Wheeler	Public Affairs	Wings to Victory
	:45	Continued	Continued	Frank Sinatra – songs	Continued
11	PM	News: Music	News	News	News Treasury Star
	:15	Music	Treasury Parade	Guy Lombardo Orch.	Parade
	:30	Uncle Sam	S.-Am. Serenade	Dance Orch.	Music for Reading
	:45	News	Continued	Continued	Music: News (11:55)
12	PM	Music: Three Suns	Dance Orch.	News; Orchestra	Music for Reading
	:15	Three Suns Trio	Continued	Continued	Music for Reading
	:30	Tropicana	News: Dancing	Signature	Signature
	:45	Music: News	Continued		

House Passes Tax Cut Bill by 289 to 67

Both Democrats and Republicans Agree Truman Can't Kill it

WASHINGTON (U.P.) – The House sent President Truman a $4,800,000,000 tax reduction bill today, pounding home its approval by a 289-to-67 roll call vote.

The margin was 51 votes greater than the two-thirds majority which would be required to override a veto.

And Mr. Truman is expected to veto the tax cut promptly, his supporters take the stand that instead of reducing taxes, Congress should maintain the current high flow of revenues to rebuild the nation's military strength in the global drive to stop Communism.

Say Veto Will Fail

But the House vote, coupled with the top-heavy 78-to-11 approval given by the Senate Monday, was viewed by Democrats as well as Republicans as assuring that the tax cut will become law.

"There is not a chance in the world that Congress will support a Presidential veto," one highly placed Democratic lawmaker said.

NEWSPAPER

Edie Elam

LOOKING AT HOLLYWOOD

All of the Columbia stars including Rita Hayworth, Glenn Ford, Evelyn Keyes, Janis Carter and Bill Holden will be featured by Sylvana Simon in "Superstition Mountain," the screen's first documentary western. The script, written by Ted Sherdeman, is from a book called "Thundergod's Gold," by Barry Storm, famous for modern treasure hunting, and deals with Superstition Mountain, once the stronghold of the notorious Geronimo, where there is supposed to be $20,000,000 worth of gold dust buried by the Apaches. Simon is trying for a May starting date.

Garbo May Play Nun

Greta Garbo will play a nun if Darryl Zanuck's persuasive powers continue to work. She is wanted for "Come to the Stable," the script Clare Luce wrote for 20th. Garbo is also Clare's choice for the part.

Linda Darnell goes into "Letter to Four Wives," most of which will be shot in New York, says Linda, "I love the part, but I hate to leave my adopted baby."

Roz Russell's had her share of illness. Her mother was sick for six months; husband Freddie had Virus X, and her son had his tonsils yanked. Roz is off to New York for a month, after which she goes to London, Paris and the Scandinavian countries. She will be back in Hollywood in August for her picture with Columbia. Said Roz, "I dare you to walk with me in Central Park." I took the dare.

Off Again

I'm off to New York for the publishers' convention, and expect to have myself a time. I'll be there for the Paul Bellamy's cocktail party; dinner with the George Camerons, of San Francisco; luncheon for the publishers' wives; the New York Daily News cocktail party at the ballroom of the Ritz-Carlton; tea with Ingrid Bergman, and a date with Henry Ginsberg to see "Mr. Roberts" and "The Heiress."

I shall miss seeing Burns Mantle, who attended the convention last year, but hope to see Mrs. Mantle, who knew three years before Burns' death that he had cancer. She never told.

Some Regrets

I regret having had to leave Hollywood before the wedding of Peggy Lloyd, Harold's daughter, and the Louis Lightons' 28th wedding anniversary party. Among those who will help the Lightons celebrate will be Theda Bara, Charles Brabin, the Brian Ahernes and the Reggie Allens. I also missed the opening of our motion-picture country hospital.

But New York was home to me long before I hit Hollywood. And, although I'm no longer geared to its fast pace, I'll do my best to limp along.

Connie Gilchrist, the fat housekeeper in "Good News," and her husband, Edward O'Hanlon, have formed a little theatre group in Santa Monica, and their play "A Kiss for Cleopatra," starring Leslie Brooks and John Lee, is a hit. This is Connie's first attempt at producing in Hollywood, but she and O'Hanlon used to have a similar group in Cannes, France, before the war.

Half A Century

"Neptune's Daughter," which stars Esther Williams, is being directed by Eddie Buzzell. This is his 50th picture. Eddie is well known on Broadway as an actor and writer. In fact, he is credited with 14 stage hits. Incidentally, he is unmarried and has a beautiful home which is loaded with antiques.

The last thing I did before taking off was send a pin-up picture of Esther Williams to a marine, who wrote: "I may never see her in real life, but –oh, brother–how I'll cherish a picture of Esther."

George Jessel swears he has done his last testimonial dinner until television comes in. "What's the use of thinking up all those quips unless America can see and hear me?" says he.

Going Strong

Sophie Tucker, the indestructible woman, whose broken leg is well, will be off to Europe in June. Her manager, Abe Lastfogel, got a 10-page letter from Sophie outlining her work for the next 14 months. Sophie is 64. And how are all you ladies doing this morning?

Seeing Spots

"Leopard People" which stars Clara Rose and William Hale, directed by Emmanuel Long, is in final blocks. This is the 7th picture starring Clara from Orpheum Studios this year. She told me how happy she is to have so many opportunities and how much chemistry her co-star, William Hale, has both on and off set.

Clara may have built her career in Hollywood, but she has her sights set on filming her next picture in England.

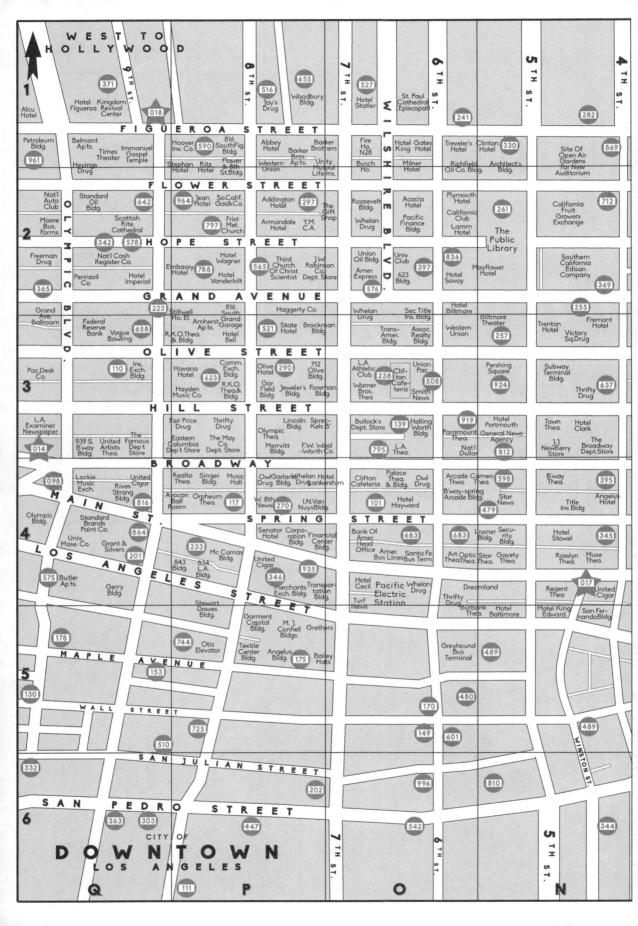

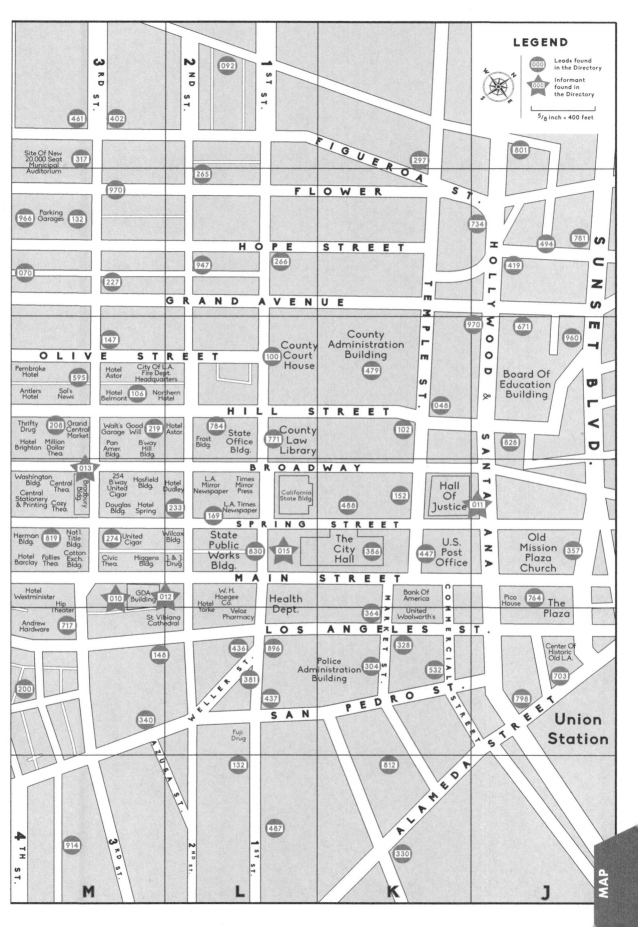

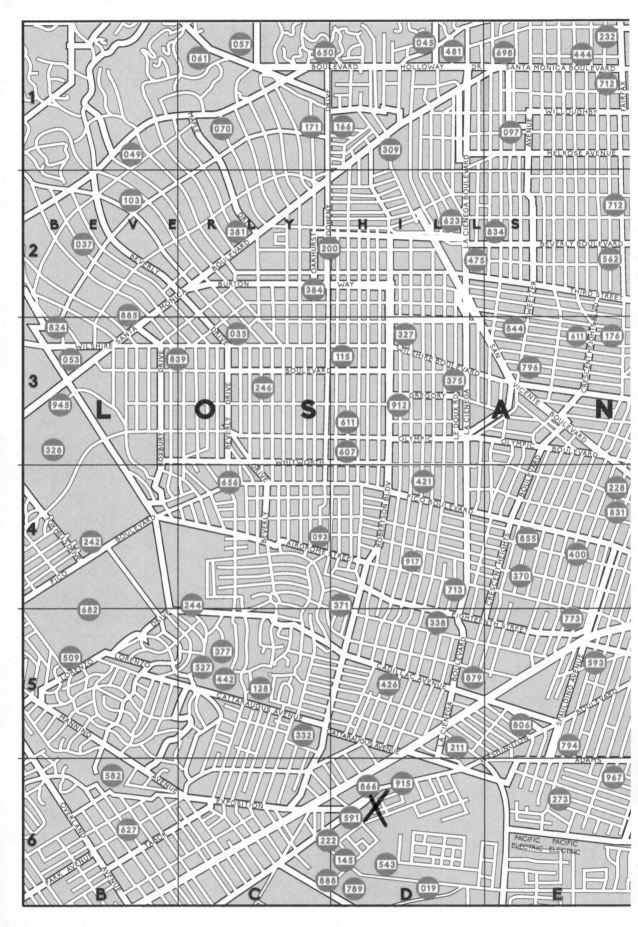

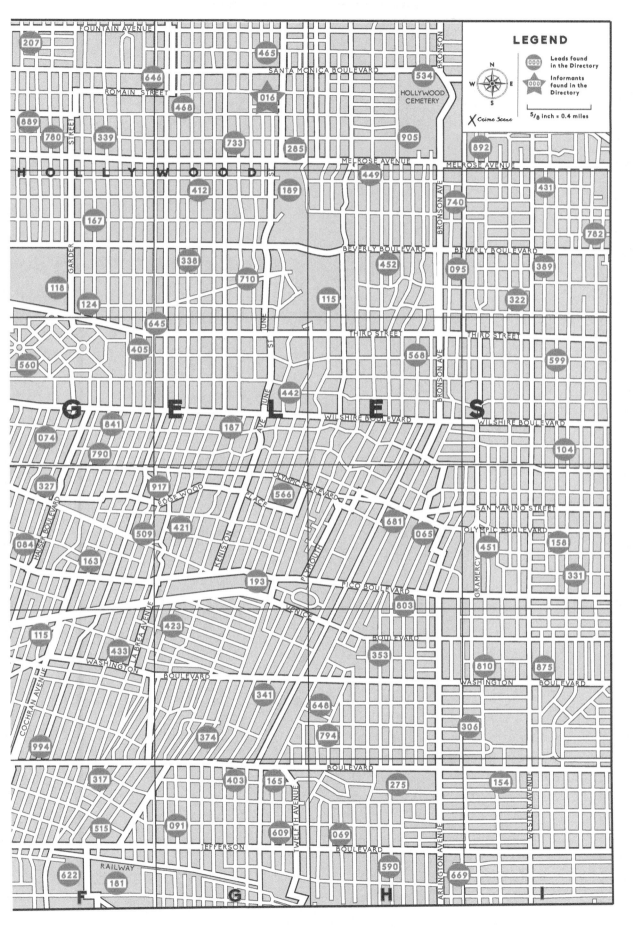

Printed in Great Britain
by Amazon

26945348R00093